THE

DEAD CLUB

By Manuel Ruiz[3]

DEDICATION

For my wife, Daisy and my son, Kristopher, who has been my inspiration since the day he was born.

Thank you both for taking this journey with me.

CONTENTS

CHAPTER 1:
THE GATHERING

My name is Grey Gomez, and I've had an unusual few days. By unusual, I mean that Monday morning at 7:03 a.m., I died. I remember the time because I felt the pain in my head weaken, then felt nothing for a second, and somehow heard the doctor read the clock.

I know people die all the time, but what made this different was that a few moments ago, I woke up. I wasn't in the hospital bed and there were no angels here to greet me like I thought there'd be, but I was definitely awake.

I was standing in the middle of nothing. The black sky, if it was a sky, held no stars or moon. The ground around me was flat in every direction for as far as I could see. A patch of brown dirt beneath my feet looked like some sort of a trail, but I wasn't sure to where.

I should have been scared, but I was more curious than anything. "Too curious for my own good," my mom always said.

Something flashed in the distance. I stared in its direction and saw it again. A light blinked every ten seconds. I looked back and saw that the trail ended a few feet behind me. I must have been at the beginning of wherever it led. I started down the path. I had to know what that light was, and it wasn't like I had anywhere else to go.

My footsteps crunched on the ground. I realized I had on my church shoes, then checked out what I was wearing. I was decked out in a sharp black suit and tie. Must have been my funeral clothes.

At least I would look good wherever I was going.

After a few minutes of walking, I saw shadows of buildings or houses forming near the beacon of light.

As I listened to my crunching steps, I noticed there were no other sounds. No wind, no cars, no birds . . .

"Aaaaah!" something screamed and then hit me from behind. I swung my elbow back as I fell and hit something that made a popping sound.

"Hey!" a voice squeaked. I flipped around and a girl in a pink dress with a pink bow in her blonde hair was sitting over me, rubbing her nose.

"Why did you hit me?" she asked as she punched my shoulder.

"You knocked me down while my back was turned," I said.

"Oh, yeah, sorry about that. Does my nose look okay?"

It didn't. I thought a few seconds before responding. "This is the first time I've met you, so was your nose crooked before?"

"No, it wasn't crooked! You broke my nose!"

"I couldn't have broken it. It would be swollen and bleeding. My best friend Kristopher broke his nose once and it bled for over twenty minutes." I was curious.

I reached over and touched the warped bone with the tip of my finger. "Does that hurt?"

"I would have hit you if it did. I feel a little pain, but it's not bad."

I put my thumb on the other side and pushed. No scream or punching followed.

"I'm going to squeeze it a little."

The girl's eyes grew big, but then shifted sideways. "I don't get it. I don't really feel anything. Go ahead, just be careful."

I pressed my thumb and finger together and felt the bone move. I squeezed harder. The bones cracked loudly and I let go.

"Keep going," she said. "It feels a little warm, but still no major pain."

I didn't hold back and squeezed as hard as I could. The bones popped as my fingers cracked. I let go and saw the sharp bend come together to form a straight nose line.

"It looks fine now," I said.

The girl tapped her nose a few times and smiled. "Feels straight."

I remembered why I was on the ground. "Why did you jump on me, anyway?"

"I don't know. I woke up, saw that light and didn't know where I was. I saw you walking and thought you might know what was happening."

"So you decided to attack me instead of just asking?"

"You might have been dangerous."

"I'm Grey Gomez," I said as I stood up.

"Grey?" she asked. "Is that because of your grey eyes?"

I nodded and smiled as I remembered my Mom explaining more than a few times how they had named me for that exact reason.

She dusted herself off and I pulled her up. "I'm Andi. Andi Lane. Thanks for helping me."

"What is that short for?"

Andi hesitated. "Andromeda. My parents were hippies. I prefer Andi."

"Then Andi it is."

"We're dead, aren't we?" she asked.

"Yes, I'm pretty sure. What do you remember?"

"I had pneumonia. I was sick for over a week. I was asleep when it happened, but remember hearing voices before I was gone. Next thing I know, I'm in this stupid dress. I only wear jeans and shorts. My mom still wants me to be three years old."

"How old are you?"

"Ten. How about you?"

"I would have been twelve in another month. Were you able to hear what the voices said?"

"No. I know it was the doctor and I heard my mom and dad crying, but everything's hazy. I'm a heavy sleeper."

I checked the beacon and it looked bigger. We were getting closer to the line of buildings.

Andi stopped. She sniffled a few times and then turned to me. "Do you hear that yelling?"

I closed my eyes and listened, but couldn't hear anything.

Andi suddenly broke into a run. I didn't have time to ask why, so I took off and was soon on her heels. We reached the first building in ten minutes. It was old and dusty and had a sign that read "TAVERN" over the front doors.

I stepped a few feet forward and saw that there were five buildings on the same side as the tavern and another four across. A thin tower about four stories tall stood in the center of everything. The beacon pulsed on top of it.

Although I'd never seen it before, the town looked familiar. I remembered seeing something like it in old movies I watched with my Dad.

"This looks like the Old West," I said.

Andi nodded. "Yeah, but it's more like a . . ."

"Ghost town," we said at the same time.

I heard voices yelling something from one of the buildings on the end.

I turned to Andi. "I hear it now."

"It's about time. Maybe you need to clean your ears."

We took off and reached a two-story building at the end of the row. It looked like a saloon with two swinging doors in front.

"Do you still hear them?" I asked.

"No, not anymore."

Something whizzed by.

I turned and saw something smash the side of Andi's head and shatter.

"That's how you're supposed to throw," a voice said from above.

A boy in a baseball cap stood on the second floor balcony. He was talking to a pencil-thin boy dressed in a blue shirt, blue jeans and blue sneakers.

"What did you do that for?" I yelled. "Do you like picking on girls?"

"She'll be fine," the boy with the cap shouted back. "It was just a ball of dirt, so mind your business."

His head snapped back as a dirt ball exploded in his face.

Andi wiped her hands on her dress and looked at me. "I can take care of myself."

The boy coughed and wiped his mouth. "Stupid girl. You would have been fine, anyway. Watch this."

He grabbed the pencil boy and threw him over the balcony railing. The boy didn't look scared. In fact, he spread his arms out like he was diving into a pool from the high board. He landed right in front of us head first. His neck snapped and his head tilted sideways. Andi and I gasped. I rushed down to check him, but I already knew there was no way he could have survived the fall.

I reached for his neck and his eyes popped open. "I'm still here."

I jumped back and fell on my butt.

The boy in the baseball cap somersaulted off the top floor and landed on his feet. He wore a full uniform that included a coiled snake on the jersey and a red belt with matching red sneakers.

"We're already dead. Haven't you dorks figured that out yet?"

Pencil Boy's neck twisted around. He grabbed his chin and snapped his head back into place.

"See, all better. I'm Jehosephant Tipton, but everybody calls me Blue. I was going to have it legally changed when I turned eighteen."

"I'd change it, too," Andi said. "Why would your parents do that to you?"

"It's a family name. My parents promised my grandfather they'd name me after his grandfather. They knew it would be tough growing up with that, so they decided to call me by my favorite color instead. They even talked to my teachers in school so they wouldn't call me by my real name. At least they were good enough to bury me in my favorite clothes. They even took care of my hair."

He patted his short blue afro and smiled.

The baseball kid slapped Blue on the back. "We found each other on the trail to the town and got bored. We decided we might as well try and have some fun. No hard feelings, little girl. You got a pretty good arm there."

He extended his hand. Andi slapped it aside. "I'm not a little girl, you jerk. But, since I made you eat dirt, we'll call it even for now. I'm Andi."

"I'm Calvin Nolan Griggs, twelve-year-old starting pitcher for the Texas Rattlesnakes. You can call me Cal."

"I guess with that name you almost had to become a baseball player," I said as I introduced myself.

"My dad raised me as a pitcher since I was three."

"How long have you been here and how did you know you couldn't die?"

"Not long," Cal said. "Once Blue and I started horsing around, I slipped off that balcony. I've broken my arm and both legs over the years, but I didn't feel much pain this time. I knew something was strange, so we started diving off the building to see who could land the best. That got old after the tenth time so we had a dirtball fight."

"Did you check all the buildings?" I asked.

Blue nodded. "They were all empty."

Cal turned his head and his mouth fell open. "Whoa."

We turned. A tall brunette with olive skin, wearing an emerald green sundress with her hair perfectly brushed down to her back, walked up to us. I couldn't help but stare at her matching green eyes. They shone brighter than everything around us except the beacon. I saw something flash on her head. She was wearing a tiara like a princess doll.

"Excuse me," she said softly. "Where am I?"

Cal, Blue and I almost knocked Andi over as we moved toward the girl.

"I'm Grey, nice to meet you."

"Cal's the name."

"Blue . . . Blue," was all he could get out.

A small set of hands shoved us aside.

"Give the girl some room," Andi ordered. "I'm pretty sure none of us have any more blood left in us, but I guess whatever boy gene that makes you stupid when a pretty girl walks by still seems to be working."

She turned to the princess. "I'm Andi, ten years old, dead and stuck here with these smooth-talkers."

The girl curtsied. "I'm Brianna Angel and I'm twelve years old. It's a pleasure to meet all of you, and I hope we can strive for peace."

She smiled and her teeth were so white they almost glistened.

"What's with the tiara?" Andi asked.

"It's my favorite one. I've won a few beauty pageants over the years and it's been my good luck charm."

"How many did you win?" Cal asked, suddenly interested in the subject of competition.

"Not a lot. Just forty-three."

"Forty-three?" Andi said. "The best I've got is winning a spitting contest. Twice."

Something exploded. A huge cloud of dust rose from behind the tavern.

We ran towards the commotion as more explosions of dirt spread into the air. Behind the tavern, a big crack formed in the ground. Each blast formed a larger crack, like a spreading earthquake. The booms continued on the far side of the buildings, and seemed to be approaching us from the other side like the earthquake was making a big circle around the town. One last blast popped in front of us and left us stranded on one side.

"It's trapped us, we're gonna fall in!" Andi said.

I jumped up and down a few times, but nothing happened. "I think we're okay."

Water filled the rift in the ground. It stopped before it overflowed and steam started rising from it. It got thicker and formed a light fog.

"It looks like a river," Cal said as he stood by the edge. He stuck a finger in. "It's warm. I wonder if we can swim in it."

He stuck his foot in the water and looked like he was about to dive in when we heard a creaking groan. The front of an old wooden boat pierced the fog.

The boat was over twenty feet long and at the back end of it a figure appeared. It wore a dark brown hooded robe and rowed slowly. Cal stepped back.

The boat stopped in front of us and the figure's head turned. It let go of the oar and stretched its arm out. A bony palm emerged.

A raspy voice spoke. "Pay the Ferryman, or spend the rest of eternity where you stand."

CHAPTER 2:
THE FERRYMAN

I checked my pants and coat. Nothing. I looked at the others. Everyone dug through their pockets, but no one had a cent. The Ferryman still had his hand out.

"The toll," he grumbled as his fingers snapped against his palm.

I felt as if the Ferryman was staring directly at me. I gazed to my sides and realized why. My new companions had all taken several steps back, leaving me standing alone. I couldn't even see Brianna.

I looked down, but felt the Ferryman's eyes on me. A soft hand touched my shoulder and I felt a mouth near my ear.

"Be brave, Grey," the whisper said, "and please don't let it kill me, if you don't mind."

Now I knew where Brianna was. The princess who had to hide behind me wanted me to be the brave one. Her dead breath still smelled sweet enough for me not to care. It made me wonder how she, and the rest of us, for that matter, managed to breathe.

The Ferryman pointed my way. "Pay now."

I stared right back at his black eye sockets. I took in a deep breath and stepped forward. "I'm sorry, Mr. Ferryman, sir, but it doesn't look like any of us have any money."

The skeleton hand balled into a clanging fist. "Come closer."

I stepped forward until my feet were touching the edge of the water. The Ferryman grabbed my tie and pulled me inches from his face. He smelled like a wet puppy.

His teeth snapped as he clenched them. "You have no payment? No coin under your tongues?"

"No," I stammered. "How could we talk with a coin under our tongues? We just have the clothes we were buried in."

The Ferryman let me go and threw his hands up.

"Nothing? You don't even have a penny?"

I shook my head. The Ferryman's head turned to the side and he pointed behind me. "What about that?"

Brianna gasped. "My tiara? No, you can't have it."

The Ferryman banged his oar against the bottom of the boat. "Why not?"

"I won this fair and square and it's mine!"

The Ferryman screamed a banshee scream, high and piercing. "You will give me that as payment and I will take you all across. Five for one, today only."

He reached out for Brianna and grabbed her hand. She pulled back.

"You leave her alone," Cal warned. He grabbed a chunk of dirt, pulled his arm back and threw it. A swishing sound cut across and something more than a dirt ball hit the Ferryman in the head.

"What the heck?" Cal's voice quivered.

We turned and saw Cal staring at his shoulder. The

sleeve of his jersey hung loosely. His arm was missing.

"That was different," the Ferryman said as he lifted Cal's arm. It was still holding the dirt ball. "This must be yours."

Cal fell to the ground. "I'm never going to pitch again."

"Come here," the Ferryman ordered.

Cal stood up and staggered. He looked like he was going to pass out, but stepped toward the boat. The Ferryman grabbed Cal's shoulder and slapped his arm back in place. It made a wet popping noise.

"There. The arm will function properly. Just don't overexert yourself."

"Is that normal?" I asked. "Are all of our bodies going to start falling apart?"

The Ferryman shook his head. "No, not normal, but nothing appears to be normal today. Can the rest of you remove your limbs?"

I tugged on both arms as my colleagues did the same. Cal was afraid to touch anything.

"Looks like we're all good," I said.

The Ferryman's form changed. He was wearing a black robe and held a scythe. "I don't understand."

"Since we can't pay, are you going to kill us?" I asked.

"No! You're already dead. I just want to do my job. People are dying, but no one's crossing over. I thought if I used my cousin Charon's old Ferryman form someone would pay me and I could take them. Not even that's working."

"What do you mean your cousin's form?" I asked. "You're not the Ferryman of the River Styx?" I had always loved mythology.

"I'm the Grim Reaper. I take many forms, but I'm usually the black robed, scythe-wielding reaper you've probably read about. The Ferryman is my cousin and had a lot of work back when Rome ruled. My reaper outfit hasn't been working today and my reaper extensions have disappeared. I didn't know what else to do."

I was really curious now. "You're the Grim Reaper. What exactly do you do?"

"When people die, I meet them and deliver them to their next stop, wherever that may be."

"And what did you mean by extensions?"

"Someone expires every few seconds. My one true form can't be everywhere, so I break into multiple reapers. In the last day, all of my extensions disappeared and it's just me, but I can't take anyone over."

"So you were supposed to take us from this town to . . . our final destination?"

"This town is new to the Underworld. I was in Purgatory, which is the fullest I've ever seen, when I noticed this town suddenly appear. It wasn't here before, so I thought this might hold some answers. Instead I find five broke kids, including one that hits me across the head with his boomerang arm. Not my best day."

"Have there been any other new towns?" I asked.

"No. Just this one."

"We must be here for a reason."

"Yes, you must."

I thought for a minute. "Is there anyone else that may know what's going on?"

The Reaper's bony hand clenched his scythe handle. "No, we will not see the Oracle."

"The Underworld has an Oracle?" I asked. "If we can't speak to him, then how do we find out what's happening?"

The Reaper flicked his index finger against his chin a few times.

"Leo can help us."

"Who's Leo?" Andi asked.

"The librarian. He is tasked with maintaining all records of the Underworld and has been the librarian for a few thousand years now. We need to see him. All of you get in."

Everyone climbed in the boat except Blue. He was staring at the water.

"What's wrong, Blue?" Cal asked.

"I don't like the water. Do we have to go in the boat?"

"No," the Grim Reaper answered. "This was just for the Ferryman charade. We can travel however we like."

The Reaper raised his scythe and an orange bolt of energy shot from the blade over the boat. The boat transformed into a long black convertible with tail fins. The vehicle had flames along its sides and "DTH" written on its front license plate.

"What is that?" Brianna squealed.

"A 1962 Cadillac Eldorado," the Reaper replied. "With my own customizations, of course."

We jumped in. I sat in the front passenger seat and Andi took the middle spot between me and the Reaper, who had his hands wrapped around the steering wheel and was wearing a slick pair of sunglasses.

Blue jumped in the back with Cal and Brianna.

I instinctively flipped on the radio. The song "Wild Thing" blared through the speakers.

The Reaper slammed his foot on the accelerator and the convertible's tires peeled out on the water, splashing and screeching at the same time. A swirling white circle appeared on the outside wall of the saloon.

The Reaper looked to the backseat. "Is this more suitable, Blue One?"

Blue raised his hands as the car sped into the circle. "Now *this* is cool."

CHAPTER 3:
THE LIBRARIAN

The car accelerated into a tunnel of multi-colored lights. I looked at the speedometer and just as we hit 100 miles per hour, the Reaper slammed on the brakes. The total travel time was about ten seconds.

"We're here," the Reaper said as he eased out of the car.

We parked in front of a single building that was two football fields wide. I couldn't see how far back it ran. There were more windows than I could count on the sides of the building. The panes stretched over two stories tall and looked like they were filled with moving clouds. Over each window sat a different type of stone gargoyle reading a book.

A big set of stairs ran up to the main doors. The stairway was surrounded in dark red brick and a flag attached to a column near the top waved and bore a picture of a stack of books.

The Reaper led us up the stairs and we all stopped and craned our necks to look at the two doors that stood at least four stories high. From the base of the doors, heavy brass knockers lined the edge of the left door every three feet or so.

"Why are there so many door knockers?" Andi asked before I could.

"Visitors can be as small as a few inches and as large as these doors. Actually, a full giant may need to crouch."

The Grim Reaper lifted a knocker and let it fall. It boomed as if it weighed a ton.

We waited.

"Is anyone coming?" Andi asked, tapping her feet.

"It's a large place. Leo needs a little time to get to the entryway."

Another few minutes passed.

Andi stopped tapping and stomped a foot. "Maybe you should knock again?"

The Reaper tilted his head toward her. "That would be considered rude and he may not answer at all."

The door creaked. Slowly, both doors opened inward, revealing a thin, frail looking man. He was bald and had a thick white moustache. He was wearing bifocals, which he was wiping with a handkerchief. He was surrounded by tall shelves filled with books on either side of him. They stretched further than I could see.

"Mr. Grim, how may I help you?"

"Leo," Grim said. "It's been what, four hundred years since I've been here?"

"Four hundred and thirty two years, actually. You really should read more."

"You two haven't seen each other in that long?" I asked. "And you remember the exact dates?"

"That's what I do," Leo answered. "So, who are your companions?"

Grim introduced us. "Everyone, this is Lord Leopold von Michelet, Librarian to the Underworld."

The librarian waved Grim off. "Please, that is far too formal. Leo is fine."

"Leo, are you aware of what's going on with the new arrivals?" Grim asked.

"I have been chronicling every soul that has passed, but it took me a while to realize there was an anomaly. I had recorded four hours' worth of names of crossovers without a destination. That's a first for my time. I thought you might be taking one of your annual breaks early."

Grim shook his skull. "I should be so lucky. Souls are coming through but not passing. I found these five in a new area."

Leo's eyebrows wrinkled. "New area?"

"Yes," Grim said. "It was like a ghost town."

"Ghost town, you say? As in Old West, Billy the Kid?" We all nodded.

"I remember the day that gunfighter's soul passed by. We knew where he was going."

Grim tapped his scythe on the ground a few times. "Leo, focus. Any idea on what's happening or why this ghost town appeared?"

"None whatsoever, but I can check our history."

Leo paced a few steps, then opened his mouth, but nothing came out. He repeated this two more times.

"What's the problem?" Grim asked.

"I'm not exactly sure what to cross reference."

"Do you have a computer?" Blue stepped forward, sounding excited. He moved toward a shelf and reached for a book.

"DO NOT TOUCH MY BOOKS!" a voice boomed, causing all of us to cup our ears. Even Grim winced.

Leo's neck had stretched at least two feet and bore thick, pulsating veins. His eyes bulged out of their sockets and his grey hair puffed up and stretched down his back.

Claws shot out of each of his hands.

Blue pulled his hand back as Leo stuck his face inches from him, revealing four gleaming fangs.

"I . . . I . . ." Blue stammered

"Blue's trying to say he's sorry," I said.

Leo's bulging eyeballs turned towards me as the rest of his face and body remained still. His neck and claws shrunk back. The little old man who had greeted us returned.

"Of course," he said. "I didn't mean to get so riled up, but it's my duty to protect the books and only I can handle them."

For a few moments all we heard was Blue's shallow breathing.

"Please," Leo said. "Mr. Blue, is it? What was your question?"

"Comp . . . computer. Have computer?"

"Those are not necessary here. I am the keeper of the books. I say what I want and the books pop out of their slots. Their titles and general contents flash in my head and I can pick and choose what I'm looking for much faster than a worldly computer, I assure you. Do you consider yourself a bookworm?"

Blue smiled and his hands stopped shaking. "Yes, the library is my favorite place in the world."

"The only drawback with my method," Leo said, "is that in this case, I'm not sure what to search for, as this is unprecedented."

"That's where a computer can help," Blue said. "If I were in the library, I'd start with 'Purgatory'."

"I have already tried that," Leo said, "but there were too many results."

"That's okay," Blue said. "On a computer you can mix words or phrases together to narrow down what you're looking for."

Leo nodded. "Very well. We need to start somewhere." He closed his eyes and softly repeated Blue's suggestion. "Purgatory."

A loud whooshing sound came from the depths of the bookshelves. The row nearest us had seven books fly out of place and hover in midair.

"Eight thousand, four hundred and seventeen books," Leo said.

Blue scratched his chin. "Let's try 'purgatory,' 'problems,' and 'crossing'."

Leo repeated the words and more books shuffled.

"Two thousand twenty six." Leo's eyes were closed and his head twitched to the side.

Blue rubbed his temple. "That's still so many. I'm not sure . . ."

Leo's eyes opened. "Disasters," he said as more books moved.

The librarian raised his palm. "I may have something."

A book flew from nowhere and hovered in front of Leo. The librarian scanned each page as it quickly flipped from beginning to end.

"Interesting," he finally said. "This has happened once before."

"And you didn't know about it?" Andi asked.

"This was before my time. Even before Grim's time."

Leo tapped his temple. "Otherwise, it would all be up here."

Grim shook his scythe. "So, what does it say?"

"This book states that four thousand, two hundred and fifty one years ago, souls stopped crossing over. It lasted for five days, then they resumed again. Something odd, though. It said a detailed account could be found in another book called 'Underworld Disasters: Volume 50.'"

Blue shrugged and raised his palms. "So, let's see it."

"That's the problem. I don't sense it, but I know where it should be. Everyone step closer."

We did as we were told.

"That's fine, now don't be alarmed."

Brianna's eyes widened. "Why? What's going to . . ."

The shelves shifted, then raced like a large wooden train moving around us. Brianna's long hair flipped and twisted in the direction of each passing case.

The bookshelves banged as they suddenly stopped.

Leo motioned to a shelf behind us. "There. That's the book."

He waved his finger, but nothing happened. "Hmmph. Book isn't budging. That's another first."

Leo snapped his finger and a ladder appeared, leaning high above the bookshelf. He climbed up five steps and reached for a black, leather-bound spine of a book, but when he touched it, it crumbled into dust.

Leo descended from the ladder with his head bowed. "Someone placed a false holder where the book should be. I have never not found a book in my library. There's only one reason this could happen. Spoken Hazard."

"What does that mean?" Blue asked.

"It means that words or phrases written in that book could cause a catastrophe if read aloud. To protect this event from happening, the book was hidden."

I didn't get it. "Who would hide it?"

"I don't know, but if it was kept from me it must be big. There's only one way to find out."

"Absolutely not!" Grim yelled.

"The Oracle," Leo said. "Only the person or persons who hid it would know, and since we have no idea who they are, that leaves only the Oracle."

"There has to be another way," Grim protested.

Cal turned to Grim. "Why are you so afraid of this

Oracle? I'll help you handle him."

"The Oracle," Leo explained, "is not a man. In fact, it is a striking woman who is one of the most beautiful creatures ever created in any world."

"Then why don't you want to see her, Mr. Grim?" I asked.

He looked down and didn't answer.

"Because," Leo said, cracking a half smile. "The Oracle is also Mr. Grim Reaper's ex-girlfriend."

"Ohhh," we all said at the same time.

CHAPTER 4:
THE ORACLE

We all wanted to ask Mr. Grim about the Oracle, but his cold stare and clenched fists on the steering wheel told us we shouldn't dare.

The car engine purred. We were all avoiding eye contact with each other when a clicking noise got our attention. Grim was tapping his fingers on the steering wheel. He reached down and pulled the gearshift into drive. The car jumped forward. We were unprepared and Andi almost flew out of her seat, but Cal grabbed her and pulled her back down.

She slapped the dashboard and her face turned red. "Hey . . ."

Cal and Brianna cupped her mouth to keep her from aggravating Grim. She was about to protest, but a bright light distracted us all. The opening that formed this time was blinding and we had to shield our eyes as we passed through.

The car screeched to a halt and I realized why the opening had been so bright. Our surroundings were gleaming. Everything we'd seen to this point had been dreary and made up of mostly black and grey tones, but now everything around us was sparkling so bright that my eyes took a few seconds to adjust. A castle stood before us that looked like it came straight from England, but instead of dark bricks, the building blocks were a piercing pink and yellow mix. The path leading to the front doors was green cobblestone and the entire landscape was filled with pink tulips.

Brianna leapt out of the back and rushed to the nearest flowers. "They're so beautiful," she said as she sniffed deeply.

The rest of us started to get out of the convertible, but Grim didn't move. I thought it was a good time to test his mood.

"How is it that this place is so full of color when everything else is so dark?" I asked.

Grim didn't look up as he answered. "Any part of the Underworld accessible to all souls must keep with the dark motif. Only a few are allowed to see the Oracle, so she can decorate her place however she chooses."

"It's way girly," Andi said. "I'd have thrown in a baseball field or a tennis court in the middle of all these flowers."

Cal patted her on the shoulder. "Now you're talking, little girl."

Grim finally turned to see the exchange between Cal and Andi. I decided to push.

"Are you coming, Grim?"

"No, you can go by yourselves. I'll wait in the car."

My curiosity was at the point where I couldn't take it anymore. "What is the deal with her? Did she break your heart that bad? Do you still have a heart?"

Grim jumped on his seat. "No, that's just it. I broke up

with her. Everything was going great, but one day she tells me she wants to be married forever. Do you know how long forever is down here? It's FOREVER. You humans get the 'until death do us part' loophole. Once you get here, you're off the hook. I was not ready for forever."

Cal clapped his hands. "I hear you, dude. Chicks can be clingy."

Grim pointed at Cal. "Yes, you get it. That's exactly what I'm trying to say."

Andi scowled and kicked one of the convertible's tires. Brianna stopped picking tulips and stood up. Her eyebrows were arched inwards, giving her an unflattering unibrow look. She walked up to the car with her teeth clenched. Blue stepped out of her way. She slapped Cal on the head as she continued toward Grim.

"So, even in the afterlife, boys are cowards. I guess things don't change."

I started to say something, but the way Andi and Brianna were staring down Grim and Cal, I thought it best to stay neutral.

Grim got back in her face. "Coward? How can you call me a coward? I'm Death, the Scythe Wielder, the One All Fear!"

"But underneath it all, you're still a brainless boy afraid of commitment. You only want a relationship when it's convenient for you."

Grim opened his mouth, but couldn't speak.

Brianna threw the flowers that were still in her hand at the Grim Reaper. "You will get out of this car, be a man and stand up in front of this woman you gave up. Do you understand?"

The mighty Reaper looked like he had just gotten grounded. His head drooped and he stepped out of the car, leading us down the green stones. With each step, the surrounding stones turned black. Brianna and Andi trailed him with their arms folded. Blue, Cal and I were smart enough to stay ten steps behind and keep our mouths shut.

The doorway to the castle was a normal rectangle shape, but curved at the top. It looked as tall as the one in front of the library, but as we got closer, it shrunk to just above Grim's head.

The door was made of clear glass, but we couldn't see anything behind it. The word "Oracle" was etched in pink across the top of the door in a loopy, cursive signature.

Grim stopped and stood at the door, which didn't have a single knocker or even a doorknob, and stared at his feet.

Brianna still had her arms crossed and was staring him down. "Knock."

Grim looked up at her. "If you want in so badly, you knock. I'm sure she'll love your crown."

Brianna extended her finger, revealing a perfectly manicured nail painted bright red. She tapped on the glass door, which started to sparkle. Blinking lights popped all around the glass and the door dissipated.

Brianna stepped into the castle and we followed, pushing Grim in with us. I was the last one through and as my back foot made it in, the glass door reappeared. We could see the light from behind us, but everything in front was black. A dim yellow light lit the small entryway we were standing in. It had red tiled floors and the bare walls were pink.

A soft voice surrounded us. "This is the Castle of the Oracle. How may I help you?"

I turned to Grim, but he didn't speak. I reached for his shoulder, but realized everyone else was looking at me. Apparently, I was the unofficial spokesperson.

"We're here to see the Oracle," I said. "Librarian Leo sent us."

"Please identify yourselves."

"I'm Grey, and I have Blue, Cal, Andi and Brianna with me."

I hesitated to mention Grim. With the little information I had on his history with the Oracle, I was afraid to say his name.

"The librarian isn't with you?" the voice asked.

"No, he stayed at the library."

"You are all new arrivals and cannot be allowed here without a member of the Underworld staff. He should know this."

I knew I had to tell. "We're not alone. The Grim Reaper is with us."

The voice didn't reply. We stood for a few minutes, unsure of what to do.

Grim broke the silence. "She's not going to let us in," he said, still staring down.

The voice returned. It sounded different, like it was out of breath. "You may . . ." We heard a deep sigh. "You may proceed."

The wall in front of us hissed as it slid into the ground, revealing another room behind it. We moved into a grand room in front of a three piece stairwell. It went up several steps and flattened, then broke into two large stairwells to either side, all the way up to the second floor. The rails along the stairway and upper floor looked like they were made of solid gold. In the middle of the flat area above the lower stair was a throne of diamonds. I had to squint when I looked at it.

"This place is magnificent," Brianna said. She stretched her neck to get a good view of the second story and her tiara fell. Blue and Cal rushed to pick it up and pushed each other to be the first to get it. I would have joined them, but Grim was in my way.

Cal snagged the crown after throwing Blue off balance. He reached out to give it to Brianna, but we all turned as we heard clicking from above.

A long, well defined, tanned leg popped out and took the first step down. The woman connected to the leg was breathtaking. I didn't realize I had drool hanging from my lip until she was almost halfway down.

The woman wore a hot pink dress that hugged her body. Her black hair seemed to wave in slow motion down to just below her shoulders. Her eyes were hazel and although she wasn't making eye contact with any of us, it felt like she was looking right at me. The best way I could describe her, and it may still not be enough to do her justice, is the Goddess of Beauty's younger and prettier sister.

Cal tossed back the tiara without looking back and it hit Brianna on the nose before it fell back to the ground.

"Hey!" she yelled, but none of us acknowledged her. She picked the tiara up herself. "Well, I . . ."

We shushed her.

The Oracle glided down the rest of the stairs, exaggerating every step. She stopped at the side of her throne and hugged it with one arm. She turned to us and gave a big smile and bowed her head. I would have given her my entire buffalo nickel collection, the one that took me four years to complete, without regret.

Blue, Cal and I finally let out our breaths. Even Andi was intrigued.

"That is one beautiful lady," she said.

"Greetings." The voice we heard in the entryway did belong to the Oracle. "I'm glad Mr. Grim has delivered you here safely. Hello, Grimmy."

My face got hot and I suddenly wanted to hit Grim in the head with his scythe. I noticed the way Cal and Blue were looking at him, and I think they were feeling the same way.

Grim just shook his head, but refused to look up. "Please don't call me that. And can you please turn the charm down a little before these boys rip each other apart?"

She blinked ever so slowly. "As you wish. I'm sorry, old habits die hard."

The heat in my face was gone. I still wanted to hit Grim over the head, though.

"You broke up with her?" Cal asked. "That was a bonehead move. She's perfect."

"He can't help that bony head. It comes with the body," the Oracle said.

"She's not that perfect." Brianna's voice was barely a whisper again.

The Oracle looked at Brianna, but instead of getting angry, she smiled and winked.

Brianna's shoulders fell. "Okay, she's just about perfect. I'm just used to being the prettiest in the room. I know, shallow, and I can't believe I'm saying this out loud."

"It's her presence," Grim said. "It lets your guard down and your emotions get the best of you."

The Oracle sat at her throne with her legs crossed. "How have you been, Grimmy?"

Grim still wouldn't make direct eye contact with her. "I've been wonderful, Oracle. Can you please just let us get to the point?"

The Oracle's cheeks flushed red. "Yes, of course. We can be all business if you like."

Her eyes started to water.

Grim turned to me. "Please tell her why we're here. Quickly."

I cleared my throat. "Miss, Mrs. . . . ."

Her lips pursed like she was sucking on a bitter straw. "By no choice of my own, it's Miss."

From her reaction I realized I had offended her. "I'm sorry, Miss Oracle. I only meant to show you respect as my mother taught me."

She took in a quick breath and her face softened. "You had an intelligent mother, then, young man. Please continue."

"We need to know what happened to the 'Underworld Disasters: Volume 50' book. The librarian told us it had been hidden and you would know why, and that somehow it relates to what's happening now. I'm also curious as to why . . ."

"One question at a time, please."

"But don't you know everything?" Andi asked from behind me.

The Oracle smiled. "Not necessarily everything, little one. I may not know something until a specific soul or creature is in my presence or asks me directly. It's important I deal with only one question so the answer in my head is clear. My reputation would be tarnished if I gave out bad information."

"So you know about the book?" I asked.

"I am aware of the book but not every detail. Leo told you about the Spoken Hazard. He was correct. There are certain passages in the book that could cause a disaster in the Underworld and the entire system of death and eternity."

"Where can we find it?"

"That's not information I can just hand over. The book was hidden for a reason. It would be more efficient if I told you how we can verify if what's happening now is the same as before, or something different."

"How?"

"Please proceed with your remaining questions first. I'm in tune now with all worlds."

I started. "The five of us appeared in . . ."

"In the ghost town," she said. "Yes, this I know."

I continued. "I want to know why and if it's connected."

"It is connected," she began.

It was quiet for a moment.

"Anything else?" she asked.

"Not yet, but I might have more if you can explain what's going on."

She didn't answer. She stared at Grim. "Grimmy, anything from you?"

The Reaper sighed. "No, Oracle. No questions."

"Oh, that's right. You tend to leave before asking the big question."

"Somebody strike me down. Anybody." he mumbled.

"Oracle," I interrupted. "What's happening and why are we here?"

She crossed her arms, still staring at Grim. She let out a sharp wheeze through her nose and turned to me.

"Whatever is happening, you five are here to help find out why and stop it."

"Why us?"

"You are connected. All of you. At the time of your deaths, something pulled you together. Just as every positive has a negative, a dark act occurred and you five are the light that can offset it."

She paused. "Wait. There is still something you haven't told me. Something's different about one of you."

I thought for a moment. "Cal," I said. "His arm flew off his body and he was able to put it right back on. Grim said that wasn't normal."

The Oracle looked at Cal. "Show me."

Cal stepped up. "What do you want me to do?"

"I want to see how your arms separate."

"I'm not really sure. It just happened."

"What were you doing at the time?"

"I was trying to hit Grim with a dirtball. I guess I threw too hard."

"Concentrate on doing the same thing. Move your arm as you are throwing something with all your might."

Cal got into a pitcher's stance and wound up, throwing his arm out. Nothing happened.

"I don't know how it worked. I was mad at the time."

"Maybe you just need a purpose." The Oracle's eyes glowed green and a platform appeared with an aluminum can on it.

"Look familiar?"

Cal smiled. "Yeah, I used to shoot cans with my BB gun at my uncle's ranch."

"Use your body like a BB gun and hit the target."

Cal's eyes narrowed. He took his stance again and flung his body forward. His right arm flew across the room and hit the can dead on.

"Oh, yeah!" he yelled.

The Oracle tilted her head. "Interesting. How did you die, Cal?"

"I'm not really sure. The last thing I remember was playing baseball in an empty lot with my friends."

"Grimmy, this is your field. What happened to the boy?" The Oracle didn't look at him this time.

"He chased a ball across the street and was hit by a speeding truck. His arms and legs were separated from his body on impact."

"Cal," she said. "Do the same thing, but try and kick your leg at the can instead."

Another can appeared on the platform. He stepped back like he was kicking a field goal. He threw his leg forward and it flew off spinning at the target. It hit the platform with a thud and the can flew off.

"That was so cool . . . hey!" Cal fell as he realized he had only one leg to stand on.

The Oracle took a moment and stared at each of us. "Each of you may have some type of ability related to how you died. Tell me how the rest of them passed, Grimmy."

Grim looked up and pointed at each of us. "Blue died after trying to make a homemade underwater bomb. Andi was hospitalized for a severe ear infection but died of pneumonia. Brianna died after a beauty contestant pushed her down some stairs. Grey died of a brain tumor."

"Have any of you noticed anything unusual, aside from the fact that you've all died?" the Oracle asked.

No one answered, but I thought for a moment. "When we were headed to the ghost town, Andi heard Blue and Cal playing when we were still really far away. I didn't hear them until we were closer. She's also sniffled a few times since we got here. Would we still be sick if we were dead?"

"You wouldn't be sick in the traditional sense," the Oracle said. "We breathe Underworld air, but it wouldn't carry any type of viruses or allergens that you would have on Earth."

The Oracle stood and reached out a hand. "Andi, please come here."

Andi walked up and took her open palm. The Oracle put her hand under Andi's chin and looked inside her ears. Andi sniffed. The Oracle flicked her fingers and a tissue appeared.

"Hold this."

Andi grabbed the tissue as the Oracle moved her index finger under Andi's nose and tickled.

Andi sniffed deep a few times and let out a huge sneeze. The tissue disintegrated as green snot the size of a grapefruit shot out and slammed against the stair rail, leaving a crack.

"Sorry about that," Andi said.

The Oracle put her hand on Andi's shoulder. "I'll have someone clean and fix that. Your illness increased the sensitivity of your ears and gave you some power behind your loose mucus."

"Wow, super boogers," Blue said.

"Your turn," the Oracle replied.

Blue stood by the Oracle and went under the same inspection. She raised his hands and squeezed. Liquid leaked from his palms.

"Why am I so sweaty?" Blue asked.

"That's not sweat. It's water. Look at that statue."

A statue of a boy appeared at the top of the stairs.

"Jimmy Taylor," Blue said through his teeth.

"You don't care for that boy, do you?" the Oracle asked.

"No, he's won every science fair for the last three years and I keep coming in second. I was trying to make a controlled explosion in an underwater tank for this year's fair. I was testing it in a swimming pool. I thought the water would protect me from the blast, but I was too close. I guess he'll win again."

"Think of that statue exploding."

Blue's eyes squeezed shut, but nothing happened. "Use a trigger," the Oracle said. "Something that will make the water in your hands do what you want."

Blue flung his hands out like he was throwing a basketball against the wall. A sphere of water formed around his hands and then broke into a stream toward the target. The statue exploded into bits as water splashed back on Blue.

"There," the Oracle said. "You can throw water bombs

if you picture it happening and then use your hands as a trigger."

"Whoa," Blue said. "That would have won me the fair for sure."

"Your turn, little queen."

Brianna walked up. "I don't want to do this," she whispered.

"What do you mean?" the Oracle asked. "Don't you want to know what special ability you have?"

Brianna looked at her feet. "I already know, but I don't want to do it."

"Why not?"

"It's not ladylike."

"Just tell me."

Brianna crossed her arms and looked down at her feet. "When that girl pushed me down the stairs, I was practicing my talent."

We were all intrigued.

"What was your talent?" the Oracle asked.

"Twirling. I know it wasn't the greatest talent, but I was learning to twirl using flames on each end of the baton. When I was pushed down the stairs, the baton went through my stomach."

The Oracle brushed Brianna's cheek. "I see now. Imagine if this ability was the talent you needed to win a national beauty pageant. Would you do it?"

Brianna's face lit up. "For nationals? Of course I'd do it."

"Then please, go ahead. You can aim at the second floor."

Brianna looked upwards, then let out a big snort and hocked a big fire loogie at the upper floor. A flaming spitball flew through the stair rails and a small fire started. The Oracle waved a hand and the flame disappeared.

"Wow!" we all yelled at the same time.

"Excuse me," Brianna said as smoke floated out of her lips.

"Grey, please come stand next to me." The Oracle stood by her throne as she waved me over.

I closed my eyes as she passed her hands over my face. They were soft and gentle. She placed her hand on my head and then back around to my face again. I opened my eyes and she was staring at me with her eyebrows crossed.

"Are you trying to hide this from me?"

"Hide what?" I asked.

She squeezed my cheeks tight and my lips pursed into a fish face.

"I don't understand," she said. "I can't read you. You died of a brain tumor and I sense that, but I can't see anything else."

"Does that mean I don't have an ability?"

"Possibly, but it's just dark. It's almost like it is being purposely hidden from me. No matter, it doesn't change anything. All of you need to get to the task at hand."

"Which is?" I asked.

"Just as your mind is dark, Grey, there is a part of the Underworld I haven't been able to see for several hours, and others I can't see at all. The Vortex Valley is your destination. Grimmy will be your guide, and the only thing left to decide is who your leader will be."

"Grey seems to be the natural leader," Grim answered.

"Wait a minute," Cal said. "I've always been the captain of any team I've ever been on. Why does Grey get to do it?"

I wasn't sure how to react. "I don't really want to be the leader."

"I do feel that it is your destiny, Grey," the Oracle said.

"So is that it?" Cal asked. "It's set in stone because you

feel it?"

"Nothing is set in stone and destinies are altered all the time."

Cal stepped forward. "I want to challenge him to be leader, then."

Grim tapped his scythe on the ground. "Combat for leadership is an acceptable challenge."

I stepped back. "I don't want to fight Cal. He can be leader if he wants to."

The Oracle shook her head. "He's challenged you, and I think it would be wise if you accepted."

Andi grabbed my arm. "Do it, Grey. You should be the leader."

"I'm not a fighter," I said.

"Fighting is not always about who is strongest," the Oracle said.

"Let's go, Grey," Cal said. "Nothing personal, but I'm not going to end my streak of being captain with you. I'll make it quick. It's not like you'll last long."

My head got hot. I didn't want to fight, but I pictured all the bullies I'd ever known in school and the cocky group of wrestlers who thought it would be funny to beat on me to impress some girls last year. I had no intention of fighting, but before I could stop myself, my mouth opened.

"I take it back. I do want to be leader, Cal. Let's do this."

CHAPTER 5:
THE TWO CHALLENGES

Cal was ready. He bent his knees and he twisted his fists as he tried to stare me down.

I hadn't been in a fight since kindergarten and it was a two punch affair. Jesse Edwards hit me on the arm and I punched him back in the chest. We both started crying and our teacher threatened to call our parents. My fighting days ended right then and there.

Cal was bigger than Jesse ever was and I'm sure he had been in more fights than I had. The only thing I knew was I couldn't back down.

"You ready, Grey?" Cal asked. "I'll be gentle."

Before I could get my hands up he ran up to me and punched me in the face. My head popped back and I grabbed my nose. I felt a twinge of heat, but it didn't really hurt. Now I understood how the boys felt when they jumped off the balcony and when Andi broke her nose.

Cal already had his hands up and was doing a victory dance. He stuck his face towards mine to gloat, and without thinking I punched him on the side of his head.

He wasn't expecting it and fell.

"I tripped," he said, looking at the Oracle and then back at Brianna. He looked more worried about impressing them than the actual fight.

I tried to figure out how that might be useful, but my thought was cut short when Cal rushed me and tackled me to the ground. He started punching my head and my face turned with each blow, but it felt like a soft slap.

"Hit him back, Grey!" Andi yelled.

"Keep going, Cal!" Blue screamed. "You got him!"

It was like they were cheering for two different football teams.

I grabbed Cal's jersey and threw him aside. I jumped to my feet, but he was already in a ready stance again. I realized he was faster and stronger and I had to improvise. I looked around for anything that might help.

"Looking for a rock to hit me with?" Cal taunted. "It won't even hurt, so what's the point? You can't beat me, Grey. I'm too good. I'll just have to make you give up."

He pounced again. He threw me to the ground and I hit my shoulder. A sharp pain dulled after a second or two. He started banging my head against the ground.

"Do you give up?" he yelled as he continued to slam my head up and down.

I didn't reply. I was disoriented and my head felt like it might fly off but there wasn't much pain. Even as Cal kept snapping my head and asking me to yield, he kept glancing at the Oracle to check if she was looking at him.

Cal twisted my arm and if felt like it was going to pop out of the socket. Then it dawned on me. The fight was almost over. I knew I was going to win and I shouldn't have to throw a punch to do it.

I flipped around to face Cal, forcing him to let go of my arm. He grabbed my hair and I threw my head back then snapped it forward, smashing my forehead against his face. He let go and I grabbed his right arm and twisted it around him as he fell face first in the dirt.

He laughed. "That doesn't hurt."

"It's not supposed to," I said. I slammed my foot into his shoulder blade and stretched his arm over to the other side of his body. His shoulder snapped like a pencil as his arm popped out. I tossed it aside.

"What are you doing?" Before he could turn back I had his left arm out, too. I turned around, planted my heel on the middle of his back, grabbed a foot, and pulled his leg up. He turned back, but didn't have anything to grab me with. I lifted his ankle and threw a hard kick into the back of his knee. His leg popped free. I pulled it through the leg of his baseball pants and tossed it aside. I did the same thing with his last leg. Kick. Pull. Repeat.

Cal flipped to his back. I turned slowly and grabbed his shoulders.

I couldn't help myself and smiled. "Give up, Cal. You can't win."

His face turned red. "I'm not giving up. Even without my arms and legs I can beat you."

His eyes shifted to the sides. I pulled him up by the hair and was about to punch his face, but I felt bad. I could almost hear my mom's voice telling me this was wrong. Cal hadn't hesitated to wail on me, but my stomach felt queasy when I thought about hitting Cal knowing he couldn't hit back.

I lifted Cal's head up and leaned into his ear. "Give up now," I whispered. "If not, I'll flip you head over stumps like a tire, and when I'm done, I'll pull your pants off in front of the girls."

His eyes bulged, but stared straight at me. I didn't blink.

"I give up," he mumbled.

I wanted to jump up and down and cheer and rub it in his face, but it didn't feel right. Instead, I picked up his arms and helped him pop them back in place, then tossed him his legs. The others came to help him.

The Oracle extended her hand, inviting me to join her. I walked up and she looked straight at me. "You ignored your pride and showed him mercy. Plus, you seem to truly care about your companions. Those are qualities that will help you become a great leader. Congratulations." The Oracle focused behind me.

I turned and Cal was coming up with his head down. He looked up and extended his hand. I shook it.

"You beat me fair and square, man. I don't like to lose, but I ain't a sore loser. That was smart how you did it. You're the boss, so lead the way."

I turned to the Oracle. "The Vortex Valley, what is it and what did you mean when you said you couldn't see it?"

"As Oracle, I need to see the past, the present and possible lines to the future. There are some spots and some minds that are dark to me. The Vortex Valley is dark to everyone. The last time souls got stuck in purgatory, whatever was responsible cast its spell in the Valley. I think that is the best place to start. Check for any evidence that someone or something has been there."

"What are we looking for?" I asked.

"Check for the embers of a fire that were recently extinguished and the bones of an animal, most likely a wolf or hyena. Something strong was called before. Something strong enough to stop the Underworld from functioning. I can't tell you more than that until we know if this is the same thing."

"The faster the better," Grim said. "Everyone get back to the car. Thank you, Oracle."

Her face beamed as she smiled from ear to ear. "Being

nice wasn't so hard, was it Grimmy? In that case, my dear, you are most welcome."

We settled back in the convertible as Grim revved the engine and the circle of light opened up. We hit the circle, but didn't come out right away. The swirling light around us kept spinning.

"What's taking so long?" I yelled over the car noise.

"The Vortex is at the edge of the Underworld. It's going to take a little longer to get there."

The white light around us darkened. A burst of lightning cracked in front of us, then lightning was everywhere. We clasped our hands over our ears, but Grim kept driving like nothing had changed. Brianna squeezed her eyes shut, but the rest of us looked all around, hoping the lightning wouldn't hit us directly.

A black flash surrounded us and the car stopped. About a hundred yards ahead was a black hole in the ground, and the air around it was spinning. It looked like the eye of a hurricane.

"We're driving through there?" Andi asked from the backseat.

Grim shook his head. "No, we have to walk. That is the Vortex. It looks flat, but it spins down like a tornado into a valley that goes down quite a way. It looks worse than it is. You all just need to step towards the center, and the air will lift you and take you down. I'll wait here."

"You're not coming with us?" I asked.

"No, my task was to lead you here. You need to make the trip alone."

"You're supposed to be our guide," I said. "You are coming with us."

"Sorry, not my destiny."

"The Oracle said destinies can change."

"You can't force me to. Now lead your people in."

I looked back at my companions. They were all scared and so was I. The Reaper had to come with us.

"Wait," I said. "Death can be challenged, right?"

Grim's eyes rolled. "Of course I can, but that deal's usually made to delay death. It's a little late."

"No, my challenge is for you to come with us and do as we ask to help on this, even if it goes against what you think your destiny is or what your girlfriend says."

"She's not my girlfriend. And what happens when I win?"

"We'll do whatever you ask and won't question it again, and we won't give you any more grief about the Oracle."

Grim rubbed his chin. "If the beauty queen promises not to lecture me about relationships again, no matter what happens, it's a deal."

I turned to Brianna. She nodded. "It's okay, I promise."

"She's good," I said. "So how does this work?"

"All you have to do is choose the challenge. I'm warning you that I've beaten a grandmaster chess player in less than twenty moves."

I turned to the backseat. "Any ideas, guys?"

"How about a baseball game or a home run derby?" Cal said.

Andi clapped her hands. "Or arm punching?"

"Or a math challenge," Blue piped in.

Each of them wanted to go with their strengths. I would have voted for a challenge on guitar or piano. I'd taken lessons the last four years, but figured Grim would be able to outplay me with his eyes closed. "No, it has to be something that isn't so common. Something he might not know about or . . ."

Brianna was adjusting her tiara. I smiled. "I got it."

Grim tapped his mouth as if he was stifling a yawn. "So, what challenge do you want to lose?"

"A beauty contest," I said. "You against Brianna and Andi. It has to have a talent, a formal dress and a girl's swimsuit competition."

Grim's head cocked back and his mouth opened. "Swimsuit competition?"

"Yes, we'll do that first and you can decide if you want to wear a one piece or a bikini."

"Wait a minute. You have to pick something else."

I shook my head. "We get to choose the challenge. Those are your rules. I'm sure you'll look great in a thong."

"Okay, okay! I am not wearing a string up my rump. You fight dirty."

"I like to think I fight smart."

The Reaper crossed his arms. "Good play, Grey. I haven't lost or given up a challenge in a long time. I am at your service. It's time to go through the Vortex. Everyone out of the car."

CHAPTER 6:
VORTEX VALLEY

We stepped to the edge of the Vortex and looked down. "How dangerous is this?" Blue asked.

"It looks worse than it is," Grim said. "That helps keep people out, and remember, you're already dead. Just watch for flying debris. Otherwise, enjoy the ride."

Grim stepped into the swirl and was quickly pulled off his feet. The air current spun him around twice. No one else had stepped in. I figured it was time for me to lead.

I waved everyone over and stepped in. I lost my balance immediately, but was held up by a soft pocket of air. I spun like I was on a juiced up merry-go-round.

"Come on, this is incredible!" I yelled at the others.

I saw two blurs as Cal and Blue jumped in. Brianna looked like she was shaking her head, but I saw Andi get a running start and push Brianna in with her. I looked back at Grim and he was gone. I was just a few feet from the black hole. The air around me was booming and grew to a roar.

"It's loud!" Andi screamed.

I didn't think it was that bad, but it must have been worse on her newly sensitive ears. I got closer to the black hole and felt my throat tighten. I trusted Grim when he said it would be safe. My feet hit the black hole first and I felt as if my body were being stretched like a rubber band as I squeezed through. I spun down the funnel below me and felt small shots smack all over my body. Small rocks and what looked like pieces of tree bark mixed together in the twisting air. I shot sideways and landed hard on my butt. It hurt for a second. I looked up and saw a thin funnel of dirt that stretched up into the sky. Cal and Blue flew by me. Brianna and Andi popped out a moment later.

Andi rubbed her forehead. "Some of those rocks really stung."

"You are all okay." Grim was behind us. "That was the Vortex, and now we are in the Valley."

Brianna was laughing hard. "That was fun! Can we go again?"

"You will all get another chance. We get to go backwards when we leave," Grim said.

We moved toward the Reaper.

"What do we do, now?" Andi asked.

"I'm just here for moral support and against my better judgment," Grim said as he placed his hands on my shoulder. "Ask your leader."

I had trouble making eye contact as everyone stared at me. "Just do what the Oracle said. We need to look for a recent fire and animal bones, or any evidence that might help us figure out if this is tied to the last time this happened. How big is this valley, Grim?"

"It would take about an hour to get across and it's mostly flat. There are patches of land with grass, dead trees and larger rocks. The vortex marks the southernmost end."

"Let's stay in one group for now so no one gets lost.

We'll just spread out and head north and stop at the places that aren't just flatlands."

No one argued. We spread out about ten feet apart and moved forward. Grim stayed behind and watched our backs.

The land was flat as far as I could see. If anything was out here we'd notice. The sandy dirt beneath us crunched with every step.

"Shh!" Andi waved for us to stop. "Do any of you hear that?"

"You've got the dog hearing, Andi girl," Cal said.

"I hear a clicking sound up there." She pointed to our left.

"Let's move," I said and broke into a run. Everyone followed. Cal turned it into a race and flew past us all. I looked back and saw Grim floating behind us. I guess running wasn't his thing, but I would be hovering if I could, too.

The ground rose ahead as we got closer. There were dead trees everywhere. Cal got there and started kicking broken bark on the ground. I heard the clicking sound now, and so did everyone else. It was coming from above.

We looked up and saw loose branches banging together.

"There's your click," Cal said.

I took a quick look around. "This area doesn't look so big. Let's check it out and meet back here."

I shuffled my feet around some dirt and dry grass, but didn't see much. After about fifteen minutes I had cleared my area and I returned to the clicking tree. Cal and Andi were already there.

"Anything?" I asked.

Cal and Andi shook their heads as Blue and Brianna returned. "Nothing here, either," Brianna reported.

Without saying a word, I got back on the original path

and we re-formed our search wall. We had only walked about a mile before we saw the second area. The excitement of the first discovery passed and this time we just jogged over. Cal still managed to get there first.

"No trees here," he said.

The area was made up of rocks and large boulders. Blue ran on top of a larger boulder that was stacked on top of others. The rocks below it separated so it made a small cave. I looked around and saw there were several cave formations like this.

"This would make a great fort," Blue said.

I had to agree. I would have loved playing with my friends in a place like this, but we were on a mission.

"Let's keep going," I said.

We moved through the opening between the rocks and mini-caves.

Brianna stopped and stared at something ahead of us. "Look at that."

Several boulders as large as houses were stacked on each other. We rushed to it and checked it out.

"This is more like a super fort," Blue said as he stepped in.

Everyone started to follow.

"Wait," I said. "I know we can't die, but if that thing caves in we could get trapped in there."

Brianna looked back. "You're right, but Grim could help us."

"That I could," Grim answered. "But it would still take me some time."

I nodded. "Plus he's not tasked to do this. How about Cal and I go in first and see if it's clear."

Everyone stepped back out except Cal. I walked in with him. The cave was the size of a big hotel lobby. I checked the surroundings, but the rocks seemed sturdy.

"Cal, do me a favor and toss some rocks at the corners, just so we know it's safe."

Cal didn't hesitate to work on his pitching arm. He went into a full windup and shattered several rocks where the top and sides of the cave met. They didn't budge.

"It looks okay to come in," I said.

Everyone entered, including Grim.

The ground was covered with clusters of rock and sand.

I scanned the area. "Kick around some of these rocks and see if you find anything."

We had fun kicking and shattering the stones. I managed to destroy three clusters before Brianna spoke up.

"I think I found something," she said.

We ran to her. Black bones were smoldering underneath the rocks she had kicked over. I picked up a still warm bone and could smell that it had been on fire.

"What kind of bones are these?" I asked Grim.

He came closer and took a better look. "Those are saber-toothed tiger bones."

I saw two six-inch fangs connected to a skull.

"Haven't they been extinct for like over ten thousand years?" Blue asked.

"On Earth, of course," Grim answered. "Even here, one hasn't been seen in a long time. I am not sure how these got here."

The thought of a tiger had me curious. "Grim, do animals have souls and do they come through the Underworld?"

"They don't have souls like humans do. They have a life force that makes them unique, and that passes through here and straight to its destination. I have no part of it. They don't appear physically in the Underworld unless they are specially summoned or created for another purpose."

Something boomed above us. Pieces of rock dust fell.

I pulled Andi and Brianna towards me. "We need to get out of here before this thing collapses," I whispered.

We rushed out of the cave as the booming continued. We turned back and saw two shapes on top of the cave's rock ceiling.

Two feline skeletons with long fangs were jumping up and down on the roof.

They didn't look extinct to me.

"Are those saber-tooth skeletons?" I asked.

"They appear to be guarding this place," Grim said.

"They can't kill us, can they?"

Grim shook his head. "Technically, no. But if they rip your flesh apart, you'll end up looking like me and it could be awhile before you put yourself back together."

A third tiger came from behind the cave.

I was getting nervous. "Grim, can't you kill them or stop them?"

"I'm sorry, Grey. I can't interfere. Coming here was your destiny. Even though I lost the challenge, there are still some rules I can't break, even if I wanted to."

The two tigers on the roof jumped down and the three of them stalked toward us.

"What are we going to do?" Brianna's voice was trembling.

A tiger leapt at Cal, but he jumped to the side and it flew past him.

I had to think quickly. "We need to use what we've got."

Cal turned to me. "I can be a target, just be sure to put me back together."

He started running full speed and jumped past the two tigers in front of us and into the cave. The cats turned around and followed him in.

I waited for a second to figure out what Cal was trying to do before it hit me.

"Blue, hit the cave with a water bomb!"

Blue lifted his trembling hands. He eased them forward but nothing happened.

"Come on, Blue," I said. "You need to save Cal."

Blue squeezed his hands into fists and then snapped them open. A water ball shot into the cave and exploded. The cave collapsed and debris flew up. We started towards Cal when something dashed by and knocked Blue down. The third tiger had pounced. Its fangs were inches from Blue's face and its bony paws had his arms pinned.

"He can't fight back," I said.

I didn't think and rushed the moving fossil. I hit it and knocked it over. One of its ribs struck me in the side and this pain lasted.

The tiger roared in my face and snapped at my neck. I closed my eyes and wondered if I'd look like Grim when this was all over. I felt a burst of heat, but no neck pain.

I opened my eyes and the tiger's bones were in pieces and burning. I heard a hiccup behind me.

"Excuse me," Brianna said.

Her fire spit had saved me.

"Thanks, Brianna," I said as I stood up. "Let's go check on Cal."

We rushed to the cave. The rocks were all broken into small chunks. I saw fresh tiger bones and realized Cal's plan had worked. The other two tigers were scattered in the rubble and sticking out of one pile, I saw a finger. I pulled it up and held one of Cal's arms. We dug through the debris. We found the other arm and Blue pulled up a leg.

"He's here," Andi said. She had a handful of hair and pulled.

"Owww, stop that!" Cal's voice yelled from below.

We dug around his hair and pulled him out. One of his

legs had stayed on. We put him back together and other than being dusty, he was fine.

"That was really brave, Cal." Brianna kissed his forehead.

Cal's face turned red. "Uh, anyone see my cap?"

Grim stepped forward and held it out. "Here," he said as he placed it on Cal's head.

"That was impressive," Grim said. "You all performed admirably."

I walked back through the rubble and dug some more.

"What are you doing?" Andi asked. "Cal has all his parts back." She turned to Cal. "You do have everything back, right?"

He nodded.

I found what I was looking for. A few of the first burnt tiger bones we found were still intact. I picked up a couple. "We have enough to show the Oracle."

"I think you're correct," Grim said. "It's time to return."

"I'm sure you're dying to get back," Brianna said.

Grim popped his scythe on the ground. "The deal was you'd stop that."

Brianna smiled. "Sorry, it just slipped."

CHAPTER 7:
CONNECTIONS

We returned through the Vortex and to the Oracle's castle and found her seated on her throne. She looked even more beautiful than the first time we saw her.

She waved me over. "You have something?"

"Yes," I said as I rushed up. "We found saber-toothed tiger bones that had been burned. Then we were attacked by three others that were alive. I mean, they were skeletons, but they moved and attacked us."

"So, your abilities saved you?" she said.

Her eyes told me she already knew all that happened.

"Sometimes it only takes a few moments of conversation for me to see some of the picture. You all did well. Let us see if this artifact speaks to me."

She took the tiger bone and ran her finger around it, taking her time. She sniffed it and then rubbed it against her cheek.

"This is definitely the same ritual that occurred several thousand years ago, but with some differences. I can't be certain if this had the same goal as the original ceremony or if it's just a clever distraction."

"Distraction? What did the ceremony actually do?" I asked.

She hesitated. "The next bit of information is dangerous and highly confidential. I am going to need all of you to give me your word that what I say will never be repeated to anyone outside of this room without permission."

We all nodded.

"You can trust us," I said.

The Oracle laughed. "To give one's word in this realm takes more than just saying so. I need an oath on your souls."

"What does that mean?" Andi asked.

"Everyone, come before me," the Oracle instructed as she stood up.

We faced her throne and she raised her hand. "To break this oath means losing your soul to the Underworld and never being given the chance to cross over. All of you are necessary for the tasks ahead, but if any of you do not want to do this, tell me now and wait outside. No one will look down upon you, as this is a high price to pay, but I must know that each of you understands what is at stake."

I stepped forward. "I understand, and I'm in."

Cal and Andi didn't hesitate. "I'm in, too," they said at the same time.

Blue took a deep breath and nodded.

We looked at Brianna. Her eyes shifted from side to side. "I'm afraid."

"Come on, now," Cal said. "We're all doing this and you need to do it, too."

Brianna crossed her arms and she started to turn around.

I moved next to her. "Brianna, we'll do this together. We all have to be a part of this, and as long as you keep your word, you have nothing to worry about. We'll protect each other."

She stared into my eyes. Even with the beauty of the Oracle in the same room, I was captivated by her deep green gaze.

"Okay," she said. "I'll do it."

The Oracle clapped her hands together once. "Then it is settled."

"What about Grim?" Andi asked. "Does he have to take this oath?"

"Like me, he is a part of this Underworld and understands the responsibility and the risk. If we were to break any of these unwritten laws, we would lose much more than our souls. Now, everyone look back at me."

She placed her palm out. My chest was hot and as I looked down, it was glowing yellow. I looked at my friends and their chests were bright, too. A blue light the size of a marble floated out of our chests and melted together in the Oracle's palm.

She closed her hand. "A piece of your soul has just been placed in the Underworld's bargaining pool, which holds you to your oaths. Now I can tell you what I know."

The Oracle sat at her throne and crossed her amazing legs.

"A race of creatures known as the Memphus was responsible the first time this ritual occurred. They are not demons or a part of running the Underworld as Grimmy and I are."

"Then what are they?" Cal asked.

"There are those that have been here since the beginning of time, such as Destiny. The Memphus were some of the original beings in the Underworld. They were around before man, when dinosaurs roamed the Earth, and well before Grimmy and I ever existed."

"So why would they do something like this?" I asked.

"The Memphus were a race of soul eaters, although they didn't intend to be. When our modern Underworld system was put in place during the dawn of man and the birth of souls, they were attracted to the strong scent and power a soul generated. Once the Keepers of the Underworld realized the Memphus were consuming souls, the entire race was given the choice to no longer exist or become a part of this land."

I wanted to hear more but wanted to ask a question.

The Oracle must have sensed my anxiousness. "What is it, Grey?"

"What does a soul eater do? I thought a soul couldn't die."

"That is correct, but a soul can be consumed by another. Although the soul itself cannot be destroyed, the character and personality that make each soul unique can be lost forever. It's the closest form of death that can be experienced here."

Andi elbowed me in the ribs. "Can you save the questions until the end, please?"

I rubbed my side as a reaction more than out of pain. "Sorry, please continue."

"The Memphus that became part of the Underworld lived in peace for thousands of years, but one of them never lost the thirst for souls. He learned of old incantations and magic and one day found a way to stop all the souls from crossing over. He took back his original form and feasted on a number of souls. I do not know who the Memphus was or how he was stopped, but I know the details were recorded in the 'Underworld Disasters: Volume 50' book. It was hidden so that nothing in the Underworld would ever find it again."

No one spoke for a few seconds as we let the

information sink in.

I replayed the words she had spoken and tried to picture what the Memphus looked like. I looked up and the Oracle was staring at me, as if expecting me to speak. "We're going to need the book, aren't we?"

She nodded. "The book was hidden on Earth."

"Where exactly?" Blue asked.

"In a place that may explain why you were chosen, Grey. It's hidden in your hometown."

"It's been near my house all this time?"

"Yes, and that may be a reason that you are here."

Cal clapped his hands together. "Now we know where it is, so let's go get it."

"It's not that simple," the Oracle said. "Once you've met Death, you cannot return to Earth easily, and even then you wouldn't have a solid body. If you found the book, you would not be able to pick it up and return it."

My mind raced. "Then what can we do?"

I felt Grim's bony hand on my shoulder.

"You're going to love this," he said. "Although your body can't physically return, you can become part of the living and use their bodies to get around."

"You mean like possessing somebody?" I asked. "Like in a horror movie?"

Grim laughed. "Not exactly. While there are spirits and souls strong enough to do that, you would ride along the person's essence. They would control their actions, but you would be able to see through their eyes."

"So," Andi said. "It's like we're piggybacking on their souls?"

Grim nodded. "Exactly. It will be necessary to find someone that you can trust. You don't want to drive them mad, so it may be easier if you talk to them first. Plus, you don't want them discussing this situation with anyone."

I already knew what to do. "I'll do it. My best friend Kristopher is like my brother. I think I can convince him to go along, plus I have this feeling that it's supposed to be me since it's in my hometown. Is everyone okay with that?"

Brianna shuddered. "Go ahead, I'm not possessing anybody. That's way over the gross line for me. I'd pick my mom but she'd keel over of fright if she saw me."

No one else protested.

"How do I do this?" I asked.

The Oracle stood up. "Grimmy and I will have to work together to make this successful."

Grim's head snapped toward her.

"Grim will take you back. Once you are Earthbound, I will guide you the rest of the way."

Grim's head drooped. "She's right. We will have to work together."

The Oracle walked over and rubbed Grim's shoulders. "I will only stay in your head as long as I have to. I promise I'll be gentle."

Grim sighed. "First, you need to make contact with your friend."

"Okay," I said. "How does that happen, exactly?"

"Mirrors are the easiest choice," Grim said. "Mirrors have dimensional properties and can be used to bridge the gap between the living and the dead. Have you ever seen a shadow or what you thought was a smudge while you're brushing your teeth or combing your hair?"

Everyone's eyes bulged.

"That was probably a spirit passing by. Now, Grey Gomez, it's your turn to be on the other side."

Grim led me outside and the others followed. We stepped on the walkway surrounded by the sea of tulips.

"Are we taking the car?" I asked.

"No, just need to be out in the stale Underworld air,

away from any obstructions. Try to keep your composure."

Grim placed his hand on my head. "Think of your friend and say his full name."

I closed my eyes and thought about our trip to Six Flags last summer when Kristopher and I rode our first roller coaster. "Kristopher Daniels."

He moved toward the flowers. "Follow me," he said without turning around.

Grim took a few steps and disappeared. I gasped and looked back at my companions. Cal gave me a thumbs up as Andi nodded.

I moved forward as I looked at the pink petals at my feet. On my fifth step, the tulips disappeared and I was standing on concrete. I heard voices. I looked up and saw a few kids playing football in the street and others riding their bikes. The trees were moving with the wind, but I couldn't feel it. I noticed a familiar black cloak standing by a tree.

Grim motioned to the surroundings. "Does this neighborhood look familiar?"

I glanced at the houses and knew exactly where I was. I was on the sidewalk across the street from Kristopher's house.

I thought of my mother and father. "I live just a few blocks from here."

Grim shook his head. "We're here for one reason only. We can't visit your parents. It would be difficult for you and we don't have time."

As much as I wanted to run to my house, I knew he was right. I looked back at Kristopher's home.

"His mother's car is in the driveway. He should be there."

"Then now's a good time. Let's go possess your best friend."

CHAPTER 8:
POSSESSION

We started across the street and walked by three boys trying to catch a football. They didn't notice us. Another boy was pulling his little sister in a wagon. As we stepped on the sidewalk, the toddler looked right at us and pointed.

"Halloween?" she asked.

"It's not Halloween, Crystal," the boy explained.

The little girl started crying. "Halloween. I want candy!"

I looked back at Grim but he ignored her. "She can see us?"

"Many young children can," he answered.

A brown dog, a Labrador I think, stopped in its tracks and stared at Grim. It yelped and ran away.

"Animals, too?"

"They can sense danger and there's nothing more dangerous than death. People need to pay attention to animals. If you see them running away from something, it's probably a good idea to follow. The curious ones who stay behind usually end up meeting me."

We walked up to the door. I reached up to knock.

"That's not going to do anything."

"Oh, sorry. Habit. So, do we just pass through?"

"Yes, we do. Just step into it. It will just feel like a soft pocket of air."

I lifted my foot and moved it toward the door. Half of my shoe went through. I felt something thrust me forward and I was through the door. Just as Grim said, it felt like a cool patch of air. I patted down my legs and torso. I was still in one piece.

I turned around as Grim came through the door. "Did you push me?"

"If I hadn't you would have taken an hour to take that first step. It is disturbing for most people the first time."

I was about to yell at him, but thought of something that had always bothered me in ghost stories. "If I can pass through doors, why am I not falling through the ground?"

Grim sighed. I'm sure he'd heard that question enough times for it to be an annoyance, but it was my first time asking.

"We pass through doors, walls and other solid objects because our spirits are not solid. Gravity still works because the ground is one of the common planes between our worlds. With effort you could touch and manipulate objects around you, but that would take some practice."

I was going to ask more about it, but then I heard a familiar voice.

"Kristopher, are you done with your homework?" Mrs. Daniels never let him play without getting his school work done first.

I headed to the hallway and peeked into the kitchen. Mrs. Daniels had her red apron with Kristopher's kindergarten picture on it. Smoke was coming off the stove and I heard something sizzling.

"Do we go to his room now?" I whispered.

"You can speak normally, Grey. They can't hear us. At least not yet."

I walked down the hall to the third door on the left. I lifted my foot and stuck my entire leg through. I looked back to see if Grim was going to push me. I turned around and I was already in the room. Kristopher was sitting on his bed, tossing a basketball up in the air. His door clicked.

Mrs. Daniels stuck her head in. "I asked if you were done with your homework. Didn't you hear me?"

Kristopher had dark bags under his eyes as he held the ball and looked at his mother. "Sorry, Mom."

She sat next to him. "Still thinking about Grey?"

He nodded.

"It's okay, son. It's only been a few days. It'll get easier. I promise. The spaghetti and meatballs will be ready in a few minutes." She kissed his head and left the room.

Grim, who had moved by the closet, focused on Kristopher's dresser. It had a tall mirror over it that was full of pictures of us playing soccer, basketball and eating hot dogs at Six Flags.

"What do I do?" I asked.

"Face the mirror and stare at yourself until you feel your insides twist. You'll actually shift into the mirror and become your reflection. If your friend is someone that is truly connected to you, he'll be able to see and hear you."

I stood in front of the dresser and stared at my reflection. I was a little pale, but then again, I was dead. My hair wasn't parted right. I ran my fingers through it.

"Look into your own eyes and don't worry about your hair. You would think you were the beauty queen."

"Okay, I get the point," I said as I dropped my hand.

I looked at my own eyes. My pupils shrunk, and then my stomach started to tingle and my hands started shaking. I got dizzy, and then I was staring back at Grim. It was like

I had flipped around instantly. I had taken the place of my own reflection.

Kristopher stood up and spun the ball on his finger. I never could do that.

"Call out to him softly," Grim said. "Try not to frighten him."

I cleared my throat. "Kristopher," I whispered.

He dropped the basketball.

"Kristopher, it's okay. It's me."

He picked the ball up again and started spinning it. "I'm not losing it, not losing it . . ."

"Don't flip out, Kristopher. Just look in your mirror. It's really me."

He closed his eyes as he kept the ball moving. "Not hearing Grey's voice. I'm just tired and hungry. Not gonna look at my mirror."

A gentle, smooth voice entered my head.

"You need to calm him down, Grey," the Oracle's voice said. "Tell him something familiar."

My head scrambled for something.

"Kristopher, don't look, just listen. I'm still gone, but this is really me. Remember when we were on that Superman roller coaster last summer? This girl in front of us smiled at you, but then you screamed like a baby during the upside down loop. We walked right past them after the ride and you couldn't even look at her, but you ended up puking all over her shoes. You swore me to secrecy and I never told anyone."

"There were a bunch of people on that ride," Kristopher said without opening his eyes. He was still spinning the basketball. "You're not Grey. You can't be."

I scanned the room. I saw a picture with a dog tag wrapped around it. The picture was of the only dog Kristopher ever owned. When we were younger, we spent plenty of afternoons running around the sprinklers with the dog trying to knock us down and lick our faces.

"Bear," I said softly.

Kristopher's head turned towards me. His eyes were still closed. "Bear?"

"Yes," I said. "You got Bear when you were five and he was our dog. We took him with us everywhere we could. I remember when we were in third grade and came home to play with him one day, but he was gone. Your Mom told us he got sick and had died at the vet. We both cried for days. That was the worst time of our lives."

Kristopher's head fell and he stopped spinning the basketball. "It was, but it didn't compare to losing my best friend." He rubbed his eyes. "I still think you're messing with me. The whole neighborhood knew that I loved that dog."

"What else can I do to prove this to you?" I asked as I continued to check the room. I saw a soccer ball under his bed.

"Soccer," I said. "We played together when we were six, and the whole season, neither one of us ever scored a goal. But on the last game of the year, I got open and you were next to me. The goalie was playing with the grass and I had a clear shot. I kicked it as hard as I could, but the ball hit you right in your face and your nose bled for two hours."

Kristopher didn't respond.

"If you want, I can try one more time."

"No, no. I'm good," Kristopher said as the color drained from his face. He turned back at me with his eyes shut tight.

"Just look at me, Kristopher," I said.

He slowly opened one eye. His eyeball shifted and he looked right at me. He snapped the eye closed again. "Mama . . ."

"Don't call your mom. She's cooking in the kitchen. I need to talk to you, Kristopher. Come on, we're still blood brothers, right?"

Kristopher and I were only children. When we were in fourth grade we made a blood oath to be each other's brother. We were scared to prick our fingers, so we picked at scabs from bike wipeouts to get the blood to swear on.

His breath shortened. "Yes, you're still my blood brother."

He opened both eyes and stepped carefully to the dresser. He moved his shaking hand to the mirror.

"Is it really you, Grey?"

I smiled. "Yes, it's really me."

"Are you haunting my house?"

"No, I'm here because I need your help. Are you calm enough to listen?"

"I . . . I think so. Are you in heaven?"

"No, not exactly, but that's part of the reason I'm here. I'm stuck in the Underworld. All the people that have been dying lately are stuck in Purgatory and aren't crossing over. None of us can move on to heaven, hell or wherever we're supposed to be. Something stopped this, and the answer is in a book that was hidden here in town."

Kristopher's eyes blinked, but he didn't respond.

"It's okay if you don't get it right now. It'll make sense eventually, but I need someone living to help me find the book. Someone I can trust."

He nodded. His lips quivered as he spoke. "And you chose me?"

"Who else?"

"Okay, Grey. I don't know how I can help."

"I need to, sort of, ride inside your body."

He pointed at me. "You're not going to possess me! Am I going to become some kind of zombie? I don't wanna eat any brains."

"No brain tacos, I promise. You'll control everything. I'll just be in your head, I guess. I'm not really sure how it works, but you'll know what's going on."

He lowered his hand and calmed down. "I guess it's okay, Grey. How do we do this?"

"Raise your hand to the mirror and have your friend do the same," the Oracle said.

I placed my palm on the glass. "Put your hand where mine is."

Kristopher did as I instructed.

I felt heat on my palm and my fingertips tingled. I suddenly felt like I had taken nighttime cold medicine and was about to fall asleep. My eyelids fluttered as I tried to keep them open. As they closed I sucked in a deep breath and felt heat in my chest. I heard a loud popping sound and I was able to open my eyes again. I stared at Kristopher's reflection in the mirror.

"Hey," Kristopher yelled. "What happened to my basketball?"

Without controlling it, my view changed. I was looking at the basketball on the carpet. It was deflated and had a big hole on the side as smoke puffed in the air.

"I'm sorry, I forgot to warn you," the Oracle's voice said. "Bodies and souls all carry a small amount of electric energy. When they cross, they let out a stronger burst."

I felt Kristopher's hands rise and he cupped his ears. "Who is that? Why's there a voice in my head? Is that you, Grey? Why do you sound like a sexy woman?"

"It's the Oracle," I said. "I can hear her, and it looks like you can, too."

This was awkward. It felt like my mouth was moving even though I had no body.

The Oracle read my mind. "It is an involuntary reflex.

Your mind is projecting what you want to say, but it feels like you are speaking normally. You'll get used to it soon."

Kristopher looked back to his reflection. His eyes were bugged out and he looked excited. "Grey! It's like hearing a radio station in my head. This is awesome."

His head flipped around as his door flung open. Mrs. Daniels jumped in the room with spaghetti noodles dripping down her hair.

"Kristopher! What was that noise?" She was gasping for air.

"S-Sorry, Mom. I . . . over inflated my basketball and it popped."

She looked down. "You almost gave me a heart attack, Son."

She patted her chest and left the room.

I couldn't control Kristopher's motions. I was just looking through his eyes and could feel his body parts moving. This was going to take a minute to adjust to.

Kristopher tapped his temple. "So you're inside my head?"

"It looks that way, but I can't control anything you're doing. I'm just watching."

"We need to find the book and a mode of transportation," the Oracle said.

"We can take my bike."

Kristopher walked out of his room and went by the kitchen. "Mom, I'm gonna ride my bike. I feel like getting out."

His mom was setting plates on the table.

She looked up at him and hesitated. "What about dinner?"

"I'm just tired of being in my room, Mom. Maybe a ride will make me feel better."

She smiled and her eyes watered. "Okay, Son. Just be

careful."

He headed out and opened his garage door.

"I can't believe she let you go just like that," I said.

"I guess my best friend dying gave me some sympathy points."

"You're gonna milk this for all it's worth, aren't you?"

"You know it. Christmas is going to be good this year."

He got on his bike and walked it to the driveway. "Where am I going?"

"Go east," the Oracle replied. "It's close, but I'll be able to gain a stronger sense as we get closer to the book."

"East?" Kristopher asked.

The Oracle sighed. "Go left."

I realized someone was missing.

"Where's Grim?" I asked.

"His only job was to get you here," the Oracle replied. "He will retrieve you when your task is complete."

"Grim?" Kristopher asked. "Who's Grim?"

I wasn't sure if I should answer, but this was my best friend. "The Grim Reaper."

"Death? Death was in my house?" I felt his panic.

"He wasn't here for anybody, just dropping me off. He's actually a cool guy."

"I think coward and deserter are much more appropriate descriptions," the Oracle said.

"Whoa," Kristopher said. "What's that about?"

"She used to be his girlfriend. It wasn't a pretty breakup."

"Death had an Oracle for a girlfriend? Is she hot?"

"You have no idea. And he broke up with her."

"Wow! He must be cool."

A gritty, not so sexy voice boomed. "I would not describe that non-committing, fashion-challenged fossil as 'cool!' Just ride before I lead you into a lake."

Kristopher pulled a hand up to his mouth as we both tried not to laugh.

CHAPTER 9:
THE BAD BOOK

We rode five blocks past the neighborhood. Kristopher turned and took a long look down my street.

I knew what he was thinking. "I want to see them, but I can't do that to Mom and Dad. How are they?"

"I heard my mom say that your dad was going back to work tomorrow to keep busy and try to feel normal. Your mother hasn't left the house."

"This will be easier if you don't know, Grey," the Oracle said. "People grieve, and the loss of a child is never easy. Your parent's lives will never be the same, but they'll find a way to go on."

Kristopher turned back to the road in front of us. I decided it was best to leave it alone for now.

"Go right on the next road," the Oracle instructed. "It's close."

We turned on the last street that was part of the Randle Creek subdivision we lived in.

"Cut through this open field."

Kristopher jumped the curb and rode through an empty

soccer field.

"I sense it is near one of these buildings," the Oracle said.

"This is Cotton High School," I said. "Where would they hide it here?"

The Oracle ignored my question and continued with her instructions. "Go between the two buildings on your left."

Kristopher turned and rode between the gym and the science building.

"Up there where the stone sign is."

Kristopher slowed and looked side to side. "What sign?"

"The one in the middle of the grass."

Kristopher stopped. He looked toward the grass and we both saw what the Oracle was talking about. A marble square sign sat in the middle of a darker patch of grass behind the science building. He rode toward it and we got off the bike.

Kristopher moved closer and we saw a series of small checkerboard tiles on the ground in front of the marble sign. Each tile bore the name of a person or family. Kristopher looked back at the sign and it was covered with a plaque that read:

Cotton High School Time Capsule
To be opened and replenished every 50 years
Senior Classes of:
1940 1990

There was enough space below the lettering to add several more class years to it.

Kristopher bent down and rubbed his hand against the etched lettering. "So, this capsule gets opened every fifty years, and then that class reloads it with stuff and seals it back?"

"That's what it looks like," I said. "Not bad since no one will touch it for 50 years. Wait, but this Underworld incident happened a long time ago and this was built in 1940."

"The book was moved," the Oracle said. "The original spot was about a hundred yards west, but it was almost discovered sometime in the 1950s. The Keepers sent someone here to move it within this capsule to ensure the spot would only be disturbed every half century and then resealed."

Kristopher shook his head. I saw the sign wobble in front of his eyes. "But someone would find it when they opened this up, wouldn't they?"

"I am sure they took precautions," the Oracle said. "There's only one way to find out."

"You want me to open it?" Kristopher asked.

"We need the book," I said. "We have to open it."

"The tile cover is thin enough that something heavy would break it," the Oracle explained. "See what you can find."

"I don't want to break it," Kristopher said. "Those names have been there a long time. What if I get caught?"

I thought for a minute. "Hey, what about your bike seat? It still pops out, right?"

Kristopher reached back. He pulled a retracting pin loose that adjusted the height of his bike seat. The seat along with the metal bar about a foot long slid out.

"See if you can dig under the tiles."

Kristopher grabbed the seat with one hand and the end of the bar with the other. He shoved it into the dirt and wiggled it around. "Yeah, it's under. It's not deep."

He jabbed the bar around the rectangular perimeter and

moved the seat sideways until the grass and dirt loosened. When he was a few inches from making it all the way around, the cover shifted.

"It's loose." He pulled the bar out and slammed it back to the point where he had started. He pushed the bar under the cover and then stepped on the bike seat, making it rise a few inches. Kristopher pulled the seat out and then dug his fingers into the dirt and pulled up. Nothing moved at first, but he crouched and used his knees to pull harder. This time the cover popped off.

A metallic cylinder bathed in loose dirt sat sideways in the hole in the ground, buried about a foot below. Kristopher brushed off some dirt and found the side of the cylinder with a lid. He wrapped his arm around it and pulled it up so that it stood upright in the hole.

The lid had "CHS" on it. Two round knobs held the lid in place. Kristopher turned them counter-clockwise until he could remove them. He then wrapped his hands around the lid and twisted it until we heard a pop followed by a loud hissing sound. He eased it onto the grass and then reached in the capsule.

Kristopher pulled out a red football jersey, pictures of the Varsity basketball team and the marching band from 1940 and 1990, and a bunch of folded letters. He pulled up three compact discs by artists Skid Row, Milli Vanilli and Paula Abdul. There were also laminated newspaper clippings about the launch of the Hubble Telescope and Presidents Franklin D. Roosevelt and George Herbert Walker Bush.

"There's no book in here," Kristopher said.

"No," the Oracle's voice said. "It's still in the hole."

Kristopher dropped down and moved more dirt. "Where?"

"Dig deeper. It's definitely still below."

Kristopher placed the items back in the capsule and set it aside. He grabbed his bike seat again and used the bar to dig a few more inches down. After a few minutes, something clanked. He jammed his fingers in the dirt and dug with his hands.

"It's just rock."

"It should be there," the Oracle said. "See if there are edges around it."

Kristopher did as instructed and used his index finger to trace a line around a smaller rectangle in the center of the hole. He shoved his fingers through and pulled up a white stone case.

"The book is probably inside," the Oracle said.

Kristopher reached around the rock to find a way to open it. "I don't see a latch or anything."

"Break it," I said.

"Won't it damage the book?"

"No," the Oracle replied. "The books of the Underworld are charmed and can withstand weather and strain."

Kristopher turned toward a concrete walkway behind us. He raised his hands and slammed the rock down. It shattered and dust flew back in his eyes. My sight went black for a moment while he rubbed the dirt out. My insides started to twist but his eyes opened and it passed.

The black eight-inch thick book sat in the middle of the broken pieces of rock. The title "Underworld Disasters: Volume 50" was etched in gold on both the cover and the spine.

Kristopher lifted it. "I'd hate to do a book report on something this big."

He reached down and opened the book to the first page.

"Stop!" the Oracle's voice shrieked. "Do not open that here."

Kristopher dropped the book and flipped his head around. "What? Is somebody coming?"

"No," I said. "The book has some dangerous stuff in it. If you repeat some of the words inside, there's a chance it could destroy the world, afterlife and all, as we know it."

"Take the book," the Oracle said. "We need to return to the house."

"I can't leave everything like this," Kristopher said. "I'm sure someone saw me riding this way. Plus, I watch those CSI shows. This is evidence someone can trace back to me."

"Hurry, then. We don't have much time."

Kristopher pulled dirt into the hole and then resealed the time capsule. He set it back down and covered the lid. It was much easier reburying it than it was digging it out. He stamped down the edges of the cover and pressed dirt along the edges. There was a mess, but the tiles and capsule were intact.

"Good enough," the Oracle said. "We need to return to Kristopher's house now."

Kristopher jumped back on his bike and sped off, holding the book in one arm and steering with the other.

As we neared the house, I saw something dark by a tree across the street. I thought it was Grim, but it was a couple of older kids dressed in Goth black. Kristopher had to have seen them, too, since I was using his eyes, but he didn't say anything. Kristopher snapped his foot down and the tires screeched to a halt in his driveway.

We rushed through the door.

"Ready to eat?" his mom yelled.

"Not now, Mom. In the middle of something."

He ran into his room and threw the book on his bed. I could feel his chest expanding. He was out of breath.

"Open the book," the Oracle instructed.

I felt Kristopher start to panic. "But you said not to."

"Follow my instructions exactly and nothing will go wrong. Now, turn to the index."

Kristopher opened the book carefully, as if it were scalding hot. He turned each page carefully. It started with a title page like any normal book, then a blank page, and finally the index. We scanned several pages. Some of the listings were "The Fire of the Ages," "Reconstructing Purgatory," "Someone Forgot the Keys to the Kingdom," and "How Not to Clean the River Styx."

"Stop," the Oracle said. "Check listing twenty-six."

Kristopher glanced down. The listing was "The Day the Souls Stopped Moving" on page 807.

"Whoever wrote this book had a flair for the dramatic," I said.

"Historians sometimes get creative when they're bored," the Oracle explained. "But they are usually accurate."

Kristopher pinched a section of pages. "Can I turn it?"

"Pay attention to the page numbers in the lower corner," the Oracle said. "Do not read any words on any page. Just find 807."

Kristopher turned the pages and was in the mid-300s. He pinched and turned two more sections and used his hand to block paragraphs so he wouldn't be tempted to read anything. He reached 796 and then went page by page until we were staring at 807.

"There it is," I said.

"Kristopher," the Oracle said softly. "I want you to lay your hand on the page, but keep your eyes on the page number. I need to get a reading on the book but I need your touch to help."

Kristopher's shaky palm rested on the page. He left a sweat stain but it dried within seconds. Even the paper was indestructible.

"I can get a mental picture of the page," the Oracle said, "but the book's protection spell will only allow me to read one page at a time. Turn to the next one."

Kristopher moved his hand and then jumped as something banged against the windows in his room.

"What was that?" he said.

"Someone knows we're here," the Oracle said.

I felt him shudder. "Someone's here?"

"Yes, and they're coming for the book."

CHAPTER 10:
MOHAWK

"Go see who they are," the Oracle said.

Kristopher grabbed the book and rushed outside without his mother saying a word. We walked to the side of the house and peeked around the edge.

The three boys in black I had seen across the street were standing there, wearing their Goth black eyeliner. Two of them had black beanies, one with a red skull and the other with a white one. The boy in the middle had a bright blue mohawk. Although I didn't know his name, I recognized him from school.

"That's that bully in eighth grade, right?" I asked.

"Yeah," Kristopher said. "His name is Jamie, but wants everyone to call him Mohawk."

Mohawk stuck his fist out at Kristopher. "You! Come here, worm food. We need that book back. Give it to us now and nothing happens to you or whoever's in your house."

"My mom," Kristopher whispered. "Grey, I can't let them do anything to my mom."

"Then let's lead them out of here," I said.

Kristopher didn't hesitate. He tucked the book under his shirt, rushed to the front yard and jumped on his bike. Dusk was settling in as he took off back in the direction of the school. He looked back and the two beanie boys were following on skateboards.

"They'll never catch us on those boards," Kristopher laughed.

He looked back again. Mohawk appeared on a dirt bike, pulling the other two with cords attached to the back seat. Kristopher pedaled faster.

He looked back again and Mohawk hit the brakes. The boarders were flung forward and were riding next to us within seconds, swiping at the book bulging underneath Kristopher's shirt.

"You should be able to knock them off balance," the Oracle said.

Kristopher kicked sideways and the kid with the white skull beanie flew off his board and into the curb.

"Yeah, that's one," Kristopher said.

Kristopher turned as a hand grabbed him by the shoulder. The red skull beanie boy had his fingers wrapped around Kristopher's sleeve.

The front tire wobbled. Kristopher tightened his grip to maintain control.

"I can't hold on," Kristopher said through his clenched teeth.

We rushed toward a curb near the school grounds.

"Pull up," I said softly, trying not to startle my best friend.

Kristopher stood on the bike pedals and pulled. The front tire jumped over the curb. The boarder's grip loosened as his skateboard slammed into the curb, sending him and his board flying.

"One more to go," Kristopher said.

Mohawk revved his bike's engine and Kristopher looked back. He was right behind, cutting through the grass. We neared the science building and Mohawk pulled up beside us. He snarled and leaned his head forward, showing a gap in his upper teeth. He stuck his hand out and pushed Kristopher's face.

We fell sideways and I felt the bike flip underneath us. Kristopher rolled a few times and then jumped to his feet. His head hurt but he ignored it. He slapped at his stomach and sides. The book wasn't there anymore. He looked around and the book was just a few yards away from his bike. Kristopher ran to it, but Mohawk was already standing near it as the beanie boarders ran up.

"You can't have the book," Kristopher said.

Mohawk picked it up. "How do you plan on taking it from me?"

"What do I do, Grey?"

"Who are you talking to?" the red skulled beanie boarder asked.

"Uh, no one."

Mohawk's eyebrows rose. "Do you hear the voices, too?"

"What do we do, Oracle?" I asked.

"Keep him talking," she said. "I can't do anything on Earth, but as much as I don't want to ask, I know someone who can."

"Yeah, I hear the voices," Kristopher said. "What did they tell you?"

"I don't know who's talking to you," Mohawk said, "but the demon helping us told us he'd make us strong and cooler than we already are if we helped him."

"I think you were tricked," Kristopher said. "That ugly 'hawk and those stupid beanies sure don't look cool to me."

"Really?" Mohawk asked. "How about saying that after we beat your face in?"

They rushed toward Kristopher and circled around him.

I felt something dark fill my insides, then felt a rush of air behind me. Everything blurred and when I could see straight, I was looking down at Kristopher and the Goth wannabes.

I could see my arms and legs. I was floating.

Kristopher grabbed his chest. "What was that?"

I guess he felt it, too.

"It's just me," Grim said.

I could still hear him in my head and he sounded serious.

"Just here to save your hide. Kristopher, you won't have control of your body the next few minutes, but you'll thank me for it."

Mohawk was standing toe-to-toe with Kristopher. The beanie boys moved to his sides.

"Our demon master will make us strong," Mohawk said. "You'll feel it when we bust you up."

The beanie boarders grabbed each of Kristopher's arms. He struggled but couldn't move.

Mohawk put the book down, then reached back and punched Kristopher in the chest.

Mohawk's eyes bulged as he almost fell forward. Kristopher looked down. There was a hole in his chest and half of Mohawk's arm was through it. His fist was sticking through Kristopher's back.

The boarders let go.

Kristopher looked back at his chest and rows of sharp teeth surrounded the gaping hole and started to close in on Mohawk's arm.

"Aaaaah," Mohawk squealed as he pulled his arm out

and stood frozen.

"How did you do that?"

Kristopher's eyes burned red and turned into a bright orange flame. "My voice is the voice of Death and the last thing you will ever hear. Would you like to meet him?"

The skin on Kristopher's face melted, revealing parts of his skull. One hand turned into a sharp blade and the other into long, rotting fingers with long nails.

"Come," Death's voice boomed. "Shake my hand . . ."

The beanie boarders ran straight into Mohawk and they all fell.

"No, we're sorry," Mohawk yelled as he crawled backwards. "We'll leave you alone, I promise! Take the book. It's yours!"

He grabbed the book and threw it forward.

"I'm not done yet," Death said.

Kristopher's hands stretched out like rubber. His rotting hand pulled off the beanies and his blade hand sliced and cut the mohawk. When he was done, Mohawk's hair was in the shape of a flower sprouting out of the middle of his head.

Mohawk and the beanie boarders were bawling.

"We're sorry!" he yelled. "Please let us go! I just want my mommy!"

"Enough, Grim," the Oracle's voice said.

"But I've still got the flying head trick . . ."

"Grimmy, I said enough. You've done what was necessary. Now go."

"Fine," Death said. "That's the most fun I've had in years. Back you go, Grey."

As Kristopher turned back to normal, my vision blurred again and I was looking through Kristopher's eyes a second later.

"Ok, what the heck just happened?" I asked.

"Possession displacement," Grim said. "When I took over his body, I had to displace you, but you had a good seat to the show."

"That stuff you did was straight out of a horror movie," I said. "Why hadn't you done that before?"

"My job got boring after a few thousand years, so I used to take different forms, or let a snake come out of my eye sockets – fun stuff like that. I ticked off one of the Keepers of the Underworld, so they added bylaws and I have to fill out paperwork if I want to do anything special. Now I usually just show up in the Reaper robe and that's it."

"But not anymore?"

"Not today. The Oracle gave me free reign on this one. Didn't really have time to warn you."

"No problem. It worked." I looked at the beanie boys. They were still trembling in fear.

"Ask Mohawk about the demon," I said.

Kristopher didn't respond. I felt his stomach twisting.

"It's okay, Kristopher. Death's done. I was floating above you. You looked really awesome. Think about it. These guys won't ever mess with you again. Ever!"

Kristopher composed himself and cleared his throat, making the Goth boys cringe.

"Tell me how you talked to the demon," he finally said.

"We . . . we were here spray-painting the school a few days ago and we all heard a voice in our heads," Mohawk said. "He promised to make us strong and gave us powers. All he wanted us to do was guard the time capsule in case anyone strange came around it. That was it."

"What kind of powers did he give you?" Kristopher asked.

"We were able to make some wild jumps on our skateboards by just thinking about it and we could hear each other's thoughts sometimes. That was it. We hadn't heard from him again until today."

"And what did he say this time?"

"He told us somebody was trying to steal a big book that was buried here and we had to stop him. We saw you leaving and followed you home."

"Ask him how he knows it was a demon and if he knows his name," the Oracle said.

"How do you know it was a demon?" Kristopher asked.

Mohawk didn't answer.

Kristopher walked up to him and grabbed him by his flower-hawk. "Do you want me to bring the knives out again?"

"No, no! I don't know. We're always talking about how we would do anything to be able to move stuff with our minds and make girls like us. I just figured this voice was a demon or spirit or something. We did what he asked, but he never gave us any more powers."

"And his name?" Kristopher asked.

"I don't know."

Kristopher tugged on the flower.

"Oww, really, I don't know!"

"He's telling the truth," the Oracle said. "Let him go."

Kristopher released the hair. "Don't you or your friends ever mess with me or anyone else again, you understand? If any of you tell anyone about this I'll cut more than your hair next time and I'll do it in front of the whole school."

"We won't," the boys all said at the same time as tears flowed down their faces.

"Get out of here."

Mohawk jumped back on his bike. One beanie boy jumped on the back of the seat and the other on the handlebars and they sped off.

Kristopher got on his bike and we headed back to the house. He held onto the book tightly and I felt his heart beating loudly against his chest.

"Are you okay, Kristopher?"

"Okay?" Kristopher said. "Dude, I'm shaking like I ate a trashcan full of chocolate. Death just possessed me. Don't get me wrong, it was way cool how I changed and scared those idiots, but I almost crapped my pants. If we don't get home soon, I still might."

Nobody said anything for the next few seconds.

"Okay," Kristopher said. "Maybe I should have kept that last part to myself."

I cackled.

"Shut it, Grey."

Kristopher held his breath and I felt him stifling a giggle. We both broke into uncontrollable hysterics all the way to his house.

"Boys," the Oracle sighed, and I could almost see her shaking her head.

For a brief moment, I actually forgot I was dead.

CHAPTER 11:
MEMPHUS BLUES

Kristopher rushed back into his room, popped the book open and flipped to page 807.

"Repeat what you did before, Kristopher," the Oracle said. "One page at a time."

Kristopher placed his palm on the page and only stared at the page number.

"Continue," the Oracle said softly.

She repeated this every five to ten seconds and continued until page 825.

"You may close the book now, Kristopher."

"Did you get everything?" I asked.

"Give me a moment to process," the Oracle said.

She hummed for a few minutes and then took in a deep breath.

"Kristopher, gently touch the book. You don't have to open it."

Kristopher placed his index finger on the book cover. The book vibrated and dissolved.

"What happened?" I asked.

"I now know all that happened according to the book and can visualize some of the events. In fact, Grey, I now know the Memphus involved in this first event and I may know how to find him. It's time for you and Grimmy to return. I have notified the Underworld Council that the book has been compromised and it has been given back to Leo until the Council decides what to do with it."

"Wait," Kristopher said. "What's a Memphus and what is the Underworld Council?"

"We thank you for your help," the Oracle said, "but I cannot reveal any more details to you. You already know more than you should."

Kristopher looked into his mirror. "So, this is it?"

I felt his heart drop. "I don't know. Maybe there's a way I can still visit you. Is that possible, Oracle?"

"Doubtful, Grey, but possible. We don't even know if the Underworld will exist after all this or how long you'll be there. I have to make Kristopher forget the book and your visit."

"No!" Kristopher and I yelled at the same time.

"Please," I said. "I understand he needs to forget the book for his own protection, but let him remember that I was here."

"He may not be able to handle that over time," she said.

"I can and I will," Kristopher pleaded. "Remembering Grey was here is a good thing. It'll help me deal with his . . . death."

He said the words as if it were the first time he had spoken them out loud.

"Besides," I added, "it's not like he can tell anyone without being committed to permanent therapy."

"Fine," the Oracle said. "I don't agree with this and if there's ever any trouble I'll return and wipe everything. If Kristopher is willing to take on the responsibility, I will do this for you, Grey. You're putting your afterlife on the line for the Underworld, so this is one small favor I can do for you."

"Are you okay with this, Kristopher?" I asked.

He nodded.

"We have to use the mirror again?" I asked.

"Yes," the Oracle whispered. "Take a moment, but hurry."

Kristopher stared back into the mirror. "It was good to talk to you and go on one more adventure."

"Yeah, it was kind of incredible," I felt myself smiling although I couldn't see my own face. "Do me one favor?"

"Name it."

"My parents. Let them know I love them and that I'm okay. Just say you dreamt about me and I asked you to thank them for always being there and that I'm fine."

"I will, Grey. If it's at all possible, please try and visit me again. This was by far one of the strangest and coolest things we've ever done. It's like we're part of some secret society of the dead or something. Take care. You were — I mean, you are — a great best friend."

"I'll always be your blood brother, no matter where I am. I have to go."

Kristopher eased his hand on the mirror. I felt him blink and then I was standing next to Grim.

Kristopher lowered his hand and sat at the edge of his bed. His eyes sparkled like a camera flash had gone off inside them and he fell back.

"He's okay, Grey," the Oracle said. "He'll wake up shortly and remember everything except for the book and the Memphus. We need to get back to the task at hand."

"Yes," Grim said. "Limbo is busting at the seams and we don't have a minute to waste."

I nodded. "We need to get back so the Oracle can tell

us everything."

"Follow me."

We moved outside the house and stood in the front yard. Grim stepped toward the dimly lit street and disappeared. I followed and on my third stride, I was back in front of the Oracle's castle. A ball of water grazed my face.

"Grey!" Andi and Blue shouted as they ran to meet me with Cal and Brianna right behind.

"Sorry about that," Blue said. "I didn't see you."

"What have you all been doing?" I asked.

"I had us all running drills on our abilities," Cal said. "Brianna didn't want to hock too many fire loogies, but everyone's doing all right with their aim and control. I can actually boomerang my arms and legs pretty darn good, too. Even caught a leg on the return once."

"Great job, Cal," I said. "That was a good idea."

Andi crossed her arms. "So, how did possessing your buddy go?"

"It was beyond incredible."

I explained all that happened with the book and our encounter with the beanie boarders and Mohawk.

"Man," Cal said. "I would have loved to have seen those guys get theirs."

"The Oracle knows what was written in the book," I explained. "Let's get back inside and talk to her."

We returned to the castle's main hallway. The Oracle was already seated at her throne and wore a belly baring purple outfit with long slits on each side to show off her legs.

"Oooh, nice outfit," Brianna squealed.

"Thank you, Miss. You do know quality when you see it."

Grim groaned. "Did you have to change to do this?"

The Oracle looked away from him. "As a thoughtless male being, you don't understand the significance of wearing the appropriate attire to match the occasion."

"So that's your story-telling dress?"

"It is today. Do you want to hear this or not?"

"Yes," I said. "Please, Oracle, tell us what you know."

"I told you before that the group of soul eaters known as the Memphus were removed from the Underworld during the dawn of man. A single Memphus was the one who found a way to retake his form and start feasting on souls again."

"By performing the ceremony with the bones?" I asked.

"Yes. The Memphus used an incantation and burned hyena bones to stop the souls from passing. This time, however, whatever did this used saber-toothed tiger bones, which are more powerful."

"What does that mean?" Andi asked.

"It means whoever or whatever did this wanted to do more than just stop the souls. I'm just not sure what."

I thought about what the Oracle had just explained. "How did they stop it?"

"It took many of the ancient beings, including Death, to stop it, but they got lucky. The Memphus was so consumed by its thirst that it absorbed more souls than it could handle and got sick. It was captured in this weakened state and The Keepers of the Underworld were able to contain its thirst and reintroduce it into the Underworld safely."

"Can't we just gather the same ancients together and do the same thing?" I asked.

"Most of those beings are no longer part of the Underworld. They either outlived their purpose or retired. For instance, Death at the time was a few generations before my Grimmy. I only know that this time around, you and your companions are the key to stopping this."

I ran over the details a few times in my head.

"Do we have any information that might help us find who did this?" I asked.

"I have a name," the Oracle said. "The name of the Memphus responsible the first time was Elvisarian."

"Wait," Cal interrupted. "His name is Elvis and he's from Memphis? Are you messing with us? Does he play guitar, too?"

"He is not *from* Memphis, he is *a* Memphus. He did go by Elvis, but that's just a coincidence. He was given another form and I know where he is."

"Is his form a hound dog, now?" Cal laughed.

"No, I think he's closer to a Heartbreak Hotel," the Oracle said. "Elvis chose to become a mountain. In fact, not just any mountain, but he's part of a recreational retreat where many of us go when we have time off."

"So he's still around," I said. "That means we can go talk to him and find out if he knows anything."

"How do we talk to a mountain?" Cal asked.

"Each creature that became part of the land would have their own way to awaken," the Oracle said. "Although they aren't really sleeping, many have become mountains or trees or dust for so long that they may not know how to communicate anymore."

"How do we contact Elvis, then?" I asked.

The Oracle's eyes blinked several times and her head tilted.

"I can't see the exact method," the Oracle said. "However, there will be some kind of sign during the Serenade that will lead the way."

"What's the Serenade?" Andi asked.

"It's a time when soothing sounds play to set a peaceful mood," the Oracle said. "Grim will be taking you to the retreat and you can all hear it for yourselves."

"So, have you been to this mountain retreat?" Brianna asked.

The Oracle sighed. "Yes, I have, although I didn't know it was part of a Memphus at the time. You might be surprised to know that Grimmy took me there on our first anniversary."

"He did, did he?" Brianna asked. "Was it nice?"

The Oracle smiled so wide it looked like her cheeks hurt. "It was one of the loveliest weekends I've ever had in my long existence. The room was beautiful. I still dream about it."

She and Brianna squealed in delight.

"Can we skip the trip down memory lane?" Grim said.

Brianna crossed her arms. "I just wanted to know a few details. It's nice to know you tried to show her a good time."

"Don't worry," the Oracle said. "You'll see it soon enough. Grimmy, it's time for them to meet Elvis."

Brianna clapped her hands. "I can't wait."

CHAPTER 12:
THE UNDERWORLD ROCKS

We were back in the convertible and Grim had the engine cranking.

"Set destination to Love Mountain," Cal said.

"The proper name is the Rock Mountain Retreat," Grim growled as he slammed on the pedal, causing the tires to screech. We flew through a white opening and immediately heard the terrain change as the tires sounded like they were crushing popcorn.

A haze of light softened the darkness. It was like being in a park with dull lampposts. There was an area the size of a stadium parking lot filled with different sized rocks, but in the background loomed a landscape of mountains that ran too high to see the peaks.

"What are those bright spots in the mountains?" Andi asked as we climbed out of the car.

"Caves," Grim said. "They emit their own light and provide privacy for guests. You can't see inside from a distance."

"Which one did you and the Oracle stay in?" Brianna

asked.

"None of your business."

"It was probably one of the tiny ones. I'll bet you're a cheapskate."

"I'll have you know we stayed in one of the upper Grand Caves." Grim pointed to two large openings that were bigger and brighter than the rest.

"Not bad," Brianna said. "Those must be like penthouses."

"My job does have its perks."

"Enough with the caves," I said. "The Oracle said we had to look for a sign during the Serenade. When will that happen, Grim?"

"The Serenade happens every day during the Underworld's dusk. It should be starting any minute now."

I nodded. "Andi and Blue, scan the ground for anything. The rest of us will keep an eye on the mountainside and the caves. Yell if you see anything."

I heard a low hum.

"It's starting," Grim said.

The hum grew steadily louder and sounded like a symphony of tubas and trombones bellowing a smooth song.

"Nice," Blue said. "Does it always sound like that?"

"The song changes each night, but they're all meant to soothe."

The music continued, but I didn't see anything. I checked each cave and the parts of the mountainside I could see.

Andi and Blue shuffled their feet and kept their eyes on the ground, but neither of them said a word.

"There," Brianna whispered. "I think I saw something in that cave."

She pointed toward a group of three smaller caves that

were on the middle left of the center mountain.

I stared, but didn't see anything. The symphony changed its melody and then I saw something flicker.

"Did you see that?" Brianna asked.

Nothing happened for a few seconds, then the music started to crescendo and the same cave flashed again. It looked like it was winking at us.

"It's like it's pulsating to the music," Blue said.

I agreed. "That has to be it. Grim, how do we get up there?"

"There is a walkway in front of each cave entrance. You'll see it as you get closer. It weaves up and down the mountain. I suggest only a few of you go up."

"Good idea. Cal, come with me. Everyone else keep looking for any other signs in case this isn't it."

Cal and I ran toward the lowest caves. The walkway was flat but rose at a slight angle. We headed up the path running full speed. When we got to the end of the lowest caves, the walkway angled up to the next level.

We kept running, but I never felt tired. I figured this must be a dead thing. Although Cal was an athlete and I was in okay shape, there's no way I would have been able to make it to the next few levels without having to stop and catch my breath.

We finally reached the three caves. Cal got there before I did. Even without being winded he was still faster than me.

I checked the cave entrance. It looked like rock, but it opened and shut as if it were a working eyelid.

We walked in, but stopped after only a few steps. The inside, which I had been expecting to be full of just more rocks and debris, looked like a nice hotel room decorated for Halloween and summer at the same time.

There was an orange couch and loveseat surrounding a

game table. The table was set up with chess pieces that looked like zombies. The back of the room held two windows twice my height and a king-sized bed decorated in dark blue sheets.

"Check this out," Cal said. "That's New York."

Behind the windows was the New York skyline at night. A few moments passed and the background brightened into deep blue water, like you were looking down from a low flying airplane. It changed again and seemed like you were staring down from space as each of the planets slowly passed by.

"Ignore the pictures and see if you can find anything," I said. "Check everything."

Cal inspected the bedroom windows and furniture and I checked the walls and couches. I looked under, around, and above everything I could see.

I ran my fingers across the last part of the cave wall. "There's nothing here."

"Elvis," Cal said, followed by a whistle and a few snaps of his finger. "Here, Elvis."

"He's not a dog," I said.

"Do you have a better idea?"

I thought for a moment. "The cave did react to the music. Maybe it can hear us if we're loud enough."

We both let out the next call at the same time. "Elllllvissssssssssssssssssss!"

The cave started to move.

"I think he can hear us," I said. "We need to make more noise."

Cal stuck his thumb and index finger in his mouth and let out a piercing whistle. The room rumbled and debris started falling from the ceiling. The entire room starting swaying, knocking me to the ground. I looked up and saw one of Cal's legs fly out of the cave entrance. The cave twisted again and both of us shot out.

We flew over the walkway and tumbled down the mountain. I hit my head a few times and a few of the knocks hurt. I landed on my back with a thud. Cal was next to me, looking around for his missing leg.

Blue, Brianna and Andi surrounded us.

"Is it an avalanche?" I asked.

Andi helped me up. "No, everything shook for a minute but you two were the only things that cave puked out."

I stood up. "Elvis, is that you? We need to talk to you!"

The mountain rumbled and the two highest caves, the Penthouse where the Oracle and Grim had stayed, popped out of the mountainside. They were connected to a long tube shaped shadow that swung towards us. As it got closer, the cave light dulled and the openings looked like eyes attached to a round head with an ever-growing neck behind it.

"Oh, my," Brianna said. "Is he some kind of dinosaur?"

"Looks like a Brontosaurus," Cal said.

"Actually," Blue interrupted, "The term Brontosaurus is no longer used. It's an Apatosaurus."

Cal gave him a dirty look.

"Although Brontosaurus is good, too."

"That is definitely a Memphus," Grim said.

The head of the creature eased down just a few feet from us. Although the neck did resemble a Brontosaurus, the face was different. The cave eyes were larger and it had more of a snout shape for a mouth.

"Are you Elvis?" Andi asked.

The snout's open end twitched. "I have not spoken for a long time. Thought I might have forgotten how. Yes, little one, my name is Elvis. How do you know me?"

Andi stepped forward. "Well, we were kind of wondering if maybe you were stopping all these souls from passing through so you could eat them all later."

She didn't mince words and I wasn't sure what was about to happen if she offended him.

"What she meant, Mr. Elvis," I stammered, "was that . . ."

"It is quite clear what she meant, young soul."

"Please don't eat us," Brianna yelped.

His booming voice seemed to rise in pitch and then sounded like he was having problems breathing. He continued and his head shook, and then he let out a big laugh.

"I won't eat you. The craving and conniving parts of me that helped feed my thirst for souls were removed many thousand years ago. I am content with what I am. Happy, lonely and troubled creatures from all over the Underworld come to me for solace and I get to hear the beautiful music every night. I couldn't ask for a more fulfilling existence."

"You did do this before, though, didn't you?" I asked.

"Yes, I did. When human souls were new, the Memphus were all overcome with a thirst for the energy they emitted. We had no idea what they were or that we were doing any harm. When the Keepers commanded us to stop, I regurgitated the souls I took and chose to become a mountain. Even so, I never lost the desire for souls. Cravings woke the conniving part of me and after many years, I discovered a ceremony that could stop the souls from crossing so I could feast on them. When I was captured, my craving and conniving traits were removed from my being. I was transformed from a regular mountain to this tranquil retreat and with my thirst quenched, I was finally able to live in peace."

I believed him. I didn't sense a hint of anger or anything that sounded like a lie.

"Grim, I think he's telling the truth. How about you?"

"I agree," Grim said. "I guess this turned out to be a dead end."

Grim started shaking. His bones rattled as his hands banged against each other.

I grabbed them and tried to keep them from moving. "Grim, what's wrong?"

"Something's pulling me . . ."

He went into a manic spasm and then flew back and disappeared. Something howled behind the mountain.

Elvis' head shot around. "See, I told you they were removed from me. I think that's them now."

"Elvis," I said. "When you say that craving and conniving were removed, what exactly do you mean?"

"The Keepers took them out of me and banished them to the darkest part of the Underworld."

"You mean they were physical things?"

"Yes, you can't just remove a sense from a Memphus. They were a part of who I was."

"And what exactly are they now?"

"I don't know. I never did see what they looked like when they were separated. But I can smell them. They're close and they're coming."

CHAPTER 13:
FAMILY REUNION

We scanned the area, but didn't see anything. Brianna was walking around and looked panicked.

"What do we do now?" she asked.

I shook my head. "I don't think there's anything we can do. Without Grim, I'm not sure how we can get out of here."

I heard a crunching sound and we looked back at the mountain. Debris fell to the ground as a shadow darted past Elvis' caves and moved down until it stopped at the bottom row.

The dim lighting around us brightened as Elvis turned his heard toward the shadow.

The shadow howled. The sound, like the mournful cry of a wolf mixed with a rough smoker's voice, grated on my ears. The shadow moved closer. Its body was similar to a wolf's, but was larger and more muscular. It also walked on claws.

Its tail was about a foot long and the end of it spiked like it had a sharpened tip.

The creature looked up and revealed a bat-like head. Its nose was flat with flaring nostrils. It had thin, dark red fur and pointy wolf-like ears. It smiled, showing off rows of sharp teeth, including two top fangs that were as long as my hands.

"Father," it hissed.

"I am no one's father," Elvis said.

"Are you not the Memphus that bore us?" a voice shouted from above.

A second animal stood in front of the highest row of caves. The light behind it made it glow.

"We were created from your essence," it said. "We are therefore your children."

Elvis moved his head up to take a closer look. "Conniver."

"Yes, I am Conniver, and you've already met my brother, Craver, down below."

Conniver had the same body shape as his bat-wolf brother, but his head was feline and his fur looked smooth and black, like marble. His face resembled a lion's, but with round, almost human eyes that were bright orange and sparkled in the light. He had jagged bones that stuck out of his shoulder blades and fangs that were twice as long as his brother's.

Elvis's head shifted back and forth between his offspring.

"You've really never seen them before?" I asked.

"No," Elvis said. "When they were removed from me, I never saw their forms. They were supposed to be banished to Tartenna, the darkest realm of the Underworld. I've always been able to sense them, but this is the first time we've met."

"They took the best pieces of you, Father." Conniver said. "We have followed your example and have stopped the dead from crossing. We've learned much more during our imprisonment and are more powerful than you ever were. We even learned how to keep the Grim One out of the way."

"You know he will come back for you," Elvis said. "No one can defeat Death."

"Not even the Grim One can stop us," Conniver said. "We can keep him away long enough to complete our tasks. Craver has thousands of years of thirst to quench and he will not be denied."

"What tasks?" I asked, ignoring the fact that I should be terrified. "I mean, what's the point of all this?"

Conniver twisted his neck sideways. "We know who you and your companions are and your purpose here."

I shrugged. "We're not even sure why we're here. How can you possibly know?"

Conniver snorted. "We know the laws of the Underworld. You are here to keep the balance. We have stopped the Underworld from functioning. If something here cannot oppose us, then something must be brought in to stop us and maintain the balance. It is obvious the living boy with the blue striped hair and his companions failed us. You found the Book and the link to our father, but it no longer matters. My brother and I have come to ensure you do not have the opportunity to catch us unprepared."

Conniver leapt down and stood next to his sibling.

"Do their souls smell sweet, brother?"

"Sweet," Craver said. "Tasty."

"My brother is one of few words," Conniver said. "His craving for souls is unquenchable and you are the first encountered. You will be a welcome appetizer before we reach the feast that awaits us."

Craver walked to the left and Conniver moved right.

"Elvis," I said. "Can you help us?"

He shook his long neck. "I have no will to fight and my body is part of this mountain. I could not help you even if I chose to."

"What are we gonna do?" Cal asked.

I was at a complete loss, but I knew we had to do something now.

"Everyone get ready to defend yourselves," I yelled. "Use your abilities."

Andi moved next to me with her fists clenched.

Cal and Blue stood ten yards away on the other side of Elvis.

I looked back, but one of us was missing.

"Brianna, where are you?" I said.

There was no response.

"Where is she?" Andi asked.

"We can't worry about that now," I said. "We have to protect each other."

Craver jumped in front of Cal and Blue.

"Attack him, guys!" I yelled.

Blue froze. Cal tried to pull his arm off, but Craver was too quick. He hit Cal straight on the chest and Cal's arm went flying as he flew back into a group of rocks.

Conniver moved towards me and Andi, keeping an eye on us with each slow step.

"This will be an easy meal," he said as a forked tongue shot between his fangs and slipped back in like a snake.

Andi started rubbing her nose.

"What are you doing?" I asked.

"Trying to make myself sneeze. If I scratch just right I can go into a sneezing fit. Ah . . . Ah . . ."

Conniver turned toward Andi as she let out a big sneeze. The lion-headed wolf yelped as a clear glob of snot smashed into his face. Andi sneezed four more times in quick succession and Conniver stepped back as each smaller blast hit him. He tried to lift his feet but he was stuck to the ground.

I grabbed Andi and we ran back to the rocks where Craver still had Cal pinned down. Blue stood next to them, still frozen.

I grabbed Blue by the shoulders. "You have to help him. Just start with a small water bomb."

Cal's remaining arm flew up as Craver continued to bite him. There was a dull blue glow surrounding Cal's body.

Blue's hands shook as he tried to form a water ball. "What was my trigger?"

"Hands," I said. "Throw out your hands."

Blue steadied his arms and a golf ball sized water ball formed in the palm of one hand. He threw his arm out and it hit Craver on his side, but he didn't react.

"It's okay," I said. "Just go bigger. Cal needs you."

His hands weren't shaking anymore and the ball was the size of a grapefruit. Blue snapped his arms out and the water ball hit Craver and knocked him back. Craver turned towards Blue and growled.

"He looks ticked off," Andi said.

"Both of you hit him at the same time," I said.

Andi sneezed and Blue hit him with another grapefruit size ball. It hit Craver on the nose and he flew back into the rocks near Cal.

"I got him!" Blue said.

I patted his shoulder. "Good job."

I felt a hot pain on my shoulder blade. My legs flew out from under me as I was flung backwards. I landed on my back and Conniver was standing over me, stepping on my chest. I was inches from his fangs and suddenly wished I had any one of the powers that my friends possessed.

I was helpless.

Conniver opened his jaws and clenched onto my chest. I felt it. The pain was hot but bearable. I gasped quickly as I felt like I couldn't breathe. Conniver pulled back on me. I looked down, expecting to see my ribs and organs in his mouth, but instead he was pulling on a blue shape. It was the same blue glow I had seen on Cal. It was like he was biting my blue shadow and trying to break it from me. He pulled harder and my head snapped back. I was gasping heavily now as I realized what was happening.

My soul. Conniver was ripping out my soul.

Something smacked Conniver on the head and he fell off me. I took in a deep breath like I had just emerged from the ocean after being down too long.

"Keep going," Cal yelled.

He was standing next to Blue and Andi, but he was still missing an arm. I looked to the side and realized he had used it to hit Conniver and it was now near my feet.

Conniver jumped back on my chest. Andi hit him with some sticky shots but he ignored them. Cal ran up and kicked him on the side. He jumped back, but kept on coming.

"Blue," Cal yelled. "You need to hit him with something bigger!"

Blue's arms expanded as the water ball grew to the size of a small tire.

"Wait," I said. "Let him jump back on me."

"What?" Cal asked.

"Just do it. Go back and tell Blue to shoot him when I yell."

Cal ran back to Blue and Andi as Conniver jumped back on and tore into another piece of my soul. I let my body go limp and didn't resist. He pulled harder. As he dug his head to get a better grip, I rocked on my back to give me some momentum.

"Now!" I yelled as I thrust my feet and arms up with all my strength.

Conniver only flew about a foot into the air, but it was enough. The bomb hit him as he went airborne and without his feet to give him traction, the lion beast flew across the air.

I stood up and watched his marble body slam into the mountain. As he hit it, my stomach felt like it had just been punched by a boxer with cement gloves. I doubled over in pain.

Andi screamed.

I looked over and Craver had knocked Blue down and was jumping on Cal.

I knew I couldn't help and that we had no chance to beat them. We had to get out now. I looked around for an exit, but all I saw was the convertible.

More yelling. We looked over and Conniver had joined his brother and had Blue on the ground. Andi was scratching her nose but wasn't sneezing. I needed a weapon.

"Andi, come on," I said.

I picked up Cal's arm and ran toward the car. Andi saw where I was headed and rushed over.

We jumped in the convertible and I got in the driver's seat.

"Do you have the keys?" Andi asked.

"No, but I don't remember Grim having any."

I pressed on the gas and the engine came to life.

"You've driven before?"

"Never," I said. "But I've been in a go-cart. Just press and steer."

I slammed on the gas and the tires peeled. I headed straight for the brothers that were trying to eat my friends.

"Hold on, Andi!"

Craver and Conniver looked up a second before I slammed into them, running over Blue and Cal in the process. The half-wolves flew back and into a cave. My side winced as I heard them land.

I got out of the car and checked on Blue and Cal. All of Cal's limbs were missing.

"My legs, my arms," he groaned.

"I have one of your arms in the car," I said. "We need to get to the convertible."

I turned to Blue. "Are you okay?"

He was shaking and breathing fast.

"Help me find his legs and arm, Blue."

We looked around and located his legs a few yards away. Blue came back with the missing arm. I was snapping his last limb together when the car started honking.

We looked back. Andi was pounding on the horn.

"Hurry! They're coming back!"

The wolves were moving full speed in a blur of red and black.

"Run!" I yelled.

We ran in different directions. Craver came at me while Conniver chased Cal.

I turned to the convertible. "Use the car, Andi!"

"I don't know how to drive!" she screamed back.

"Just press and go."

Craver nipped my heel and I fell.

"I can't reach the pedals!"

Craver chomped into my back right before the roar of the convertible flew by, but the bat-wolf jumped before he could be hit. I got up and dove into the back seat.

Andi was sitting in the driver's seat, smiling.

"How did you reach the pedal?" I asked.

She lifted up Cal's arm and the car slowed. "This came in handy."

She flung the arm back down and sped up. We rushed towards Blue who was hiding by some rocks and he got in the front seat. Andi made a spinning turn and we moved toward Cal.

Cal was waving his arm to keep Conniver back, then took off running.

"Get the car between them," I said.

Andi steered the car and cut Conniver off. I reached out and pulled Cal in the backseat as something hit me from behind.

I turned and saw a familiar face.

"Brianna, where have you been?"

She looked down. Her eyes were watery and she was trembling. She crouched behind the seat and stuck her head down.

I tapped Andi on the shoulder. "We're all here. Hit it, Andi," I said.

She turned and slammed on the pedal again, but Conniver jumped on the trunk and dug his claws in the metal.

"Grim," I said aloud. "If you can hear me, please get us a portal. We'll drive out of here, but need your help."

I looked around as Andi steered the car into a repeating doughnut.

Conniver was still inching up the car. I reached back and punched him in the face, but he didn't flinch. His eyes sparkled, but behind him I saw something flash.

There was a pulsating white circle, no bigger than a hubcap.

"Andi, the portal's opening! Go as fast as you can."

She turned the car toward the light and sped toward it.

Conniver started swiping and just missed my head.

"We gotta get him off the car or we'll bring him with us," I told Cal.

He helped me punch, but nothing happened.

"Find a weak spot," Cal said.

I noticed Conniver's large lion nose. I looked at Cal and raised my index and middle finger together.

I turned and shoved my fingers into one of Conniver's nostrils. It went in deep and I twisted my hand around, feeling the wet muck inside.

Cal did the same with the other nostril. The beast snorted and fell off the car as we flashed through the gateway.

We had escaped the Sons of Elvis.

CHAPTER 14:
SEARCH

We emerged from the gateway in front of the Oracle's castle. It was getting closer fast.

We raced up the walkway toward the entrance. The car wasn't slowing down.

I tried to remain as calm as I could as I leaned forward. "Andi, now's a good time to stop the car."

The car flattened a patch of pink tulips.

I jumped to the front and saw the problem. Andi had Cal's arm jammed between the gas and the bottom of the seat. I wrapped my arm around Cal's arm and pulled.

"Hit the brakes!" I yelled.

"I can't reach the brakes, either!" she screamed back at me.

Cal leapt up over Andi and grabbed the steering wheel, knocking her forward. She hit the brakes with both feet as she slid down.

The tires squealed and the car hit the front of the castle steps. We jerked forward and came to a full stop.

We were all breathing heavy. I saw Brianna still

crouching on the back floorboard, whimpering.

I got out of the car and checked the convertible damage. The front bumper was scrunched in and the hood had a small dent, but the rest of the car looked intact.

"Could have been worse," Cal said.

Everyone but Brianna got out of the car.

"Grim opened that gateway for us," I said. "He must be inside."

Brianna sat up in the backseat.

"Come on, Brianna," I said. "It's okay."

She walked out of the car, but kept her eyes at her feet.

"Let's go," Cal said.

We ran up the steps and into the Oracle's main hallway. She wasn't there.

We heard something fall from above and then the Oracle came running down the stairway. She was sweating and one of her shoes flew off before she reached the bottom.

She looked around and behind us. "Where is he?"

We looked at each other.

"Grimmy?" she said. "Where's my Grimmy?"

"We were attacked and he opened a gateway for us," I said. "Since we ended up here I thought he'd be with you."

"No, something's wrong. I felt a distress vibe from him."

The Oracle rushed towards us and then grabbed Brianna's hand. She was trying to get a read on what had happened.

"Craver and Conniver," she whispered. "They found a way to get rid of him so he wouldn't interfere when they tried to destroy you, but you all fought bravely and found a way out."

"We were lucky," I said.

"And we didn't ALL fight," Andi said. "Some of us

thought hiding would help."

Brianna's mouth trembled. "I'm sorry. I was so scared. I . . . I didn't know what to do."

"It's okay, Brianna," I said. "It was all my fault. I didn't know what to do, either. I almost cost us all our souls."

"Don't take the blame, Grey," Andi said. "She didn't even . . ."

"I don't have a power like she does," I said. "What good was I?"

"You used the car to get us out."

"That was just luck. If Grim hadn't opened the gateway or if you, Blue and Cal hadn't used your abilities to fight, we would have never made it. I was useless. Oracle, I want to give up being the group's leader. I think Cal should be the one."

The Oracle crossed her arms. "My Grimmy is missing. We don't have time for this."

"Fine," I said. "Cal is the leader. Let's not waste time discussing it."

"You would abandon your companions?" the Oracle asked.

"No, I will still be a part of this, but how can I look any of them in the eye when I almost got us all killed when it mattered most?"

Cal finished adjusting his arm and then moved in front of me, wearing a big smile.

"Grey," he said. "I would love to be the leader, but let me tell you something. I've been an all-star pitcher every year that I've played ball. Two years ago, I went up against this guy, Michael Rios. The kid was half my size and looked like he couldn't play kickball, but he got on the mound and destroyed our team. As tough as it was to admit, he was better than me, and I knew it."

I shook my head. "But I can't pitch, Cal."

"Not true. You pitched a better game a little while ago than I ever could have. I might have fought hard out there, but you know what I was thinking when that bat-thing was on me? I was thinking about hitting back and fighting until I couldn't fight anymore. That whole time you were the only one trying to figure out how to save us all. I could have fought for maybe another five or ten minutes, but I know I would have lost. I don't care if we were lucky or if you have abilities or not, but I know we need you to lead us."

The others moved and stood beside Cal. He extended his hand to me. I hesitated a moment, then reached out and shook it.

"Does anybody object?" Cal asked.

Andi and Blue put their hands on ours.

Brianna stood to the side. "I know I didn't help during that fight, but I would never have come this far if it wasn't for you, Grey. Please stay and I promise I'll try harder next time."

She laid her hand with the rest of us.

I felt a lump in my throat start to throb.

"Okay," I whispered. "I'll lead you. Thanks, guys."

"Now, that settles everything," the Oracle said. "Can we please get back to finding my Grimmy? I think I might know where he is, but we need to go now if we have any chance of saving him."

The Oracle rushed outside the castle. By the time we made it down the steps she was sitting in the driver's seat of the slightly damaged convertible. She brushed her hair back with her hands and we all stood and stared for a moment.

"Get in, please," she said, almost singing.

I was in front and reached the passenger seat first. Andi squeezed in the middle and the rest jumped in the back.

The Oracle backed up, then hit the gas and her hair danced in the wind as the car leapt forward. Although I had already spent time with the Oracle, I still couldn't keep my eyes off her.

We hit the gateway and then stopped. It took me a few seconds to break eye contact from the Oracle's face. I checked the rest of the car and noticed everyone was entranced by her.

"I know you're a hottie and all," Brianna said, "But I couldn't stop staring at you. Did you do that on purpose?"

The Oracle laughed. "I'm sorry. I don't get out of the castle that often and I haven't driven in a long time. My senses tend to spill over when I'm excited or upset. I didn't mean to mesmerize you, but I can't say I didn't enjoy it."

We got out of the car and looked at the endless horizon of black and dark green water before us. The patches of black looked like small islands scattered throughout the water.

"What is this place?" I asked.

"This is Tar Lake," the Oracle said. "This is how to get to Tartenna."

"Tartenna?" I asked. "Elvis said that's where Craver and Conniver were banished to. You think Grim's there?"

"Yes. The Sons of Elvis found a way out and it is the smartest place for them to have sent Grim. He would be incapacitated there."

"So, how do we get across?" Cal asked.

"There is no direct way and the path and method of transportation can change each time. You have to state a destination and will be shown the way. Usually a boat or some type of creature appears to take you across."

"I hope it's a yacht," Brianna said.

I walked up to the water's edge and felt the black sand at my feet. I cleared my throat.

"We need to get to Tartenna."

My voice echoed and the water near me rippled with each word I spoke. A green light emerged from the water and floated toward us. It pulsed like it had a heartbeat.

"You may not pass," the orb said.

The Oracle stepped forward. "I am the Oracle of the Underworld, and I shall pass."

The orb continued pulsating but didn't respond.

The Oracle's eyes flared as she moved toward the orb, then she dug her feet into the sand and stopped. She lifted her hands and her palms flattened against the air like they were pressing against a glass door.

She dropped her hands and glared at the orb. "Why can't I move closer?"

"All Underworlders are forbidden entry."

"Forbidden? Let me through!"

"It pains me to deny your beauty, but an enchantment is in place that I cannot undo."

I reached forward, but didn't feel anything. I took a few more steps and my foot landed in the water.

The orb pulsed faster.

"You are somehow immune to the enchantment," the Oracle said. "I suspect that all of you are."

Cal moved up and the rest joined him until they were all next to me with their ankles in the lake.

The Oracle took a few steps back and then addressed the orb. "Guide, lead them to Tartenna."

"You dare to take the path?" the orb asked.

"I don't see a path," Cal said.

"It is underneath the blackness of Tar Lake," the orb said.

"No one has ever had to travel underwater," the Oracle said. "Where is the transport?"

"The sons of the Memphus disabled all travel vessels,"

the orb said. "This is the only way."

The orb floated below the water surface. It pulsed, waiting.

"Are we supposed to swim all the way across?" Cal asked. "I'm a good swimmer, but how far is this?"

"I'm not ready to get back in the water. Last time didn't work out so great for me, considering I ended up here," Blue said.

"And I can't swim," Andi said.

Cal snorted. "Why does it matter? We're already dead, so it's not like we can drown."

"Actually," the Oracle said. "Although you can't drown, the tar in this lake would still fill your essence. It would weigh you down and you'd sink to the bottom."

"How deep is that?" Blue asked.

"Some parts are considered bottomless."

"You three go without us," Andi said.

I shook my head. "No. We don't know what's out there and we all have to go."

"Do you have a submarine in your pocket I don't know about?" Cal asked.

I thought for a moment. "No, no submarine, but we can improvise. Blue, how big can you make those water bombs?"

Blue shrugged. "I'm not sure."

He held his hands together and the water bomb in his hand was about the size of a kickball.

"Bigger," I said. "We need bigger."

He tried again and it was about twice as big. I eased my hand in and through. It was pure water.

"Can you hollow this out?" I asked.

"What do you mean?"

"Like a bubble," I said. "Water on the outside, empty on the inside. Just try it."

"Bubble," Blue mumbled as he massaged the water ball in his hands.

"I think I got it," he said.

I put my hand back in. It was wet until my knuckles passed through. I sensed the empty center with my fingertips.

"Just like that, Blue. Now, we just need it to be bigger than we are."

"I get it," Andi said. "It has to be big enough for all of us to fit inside, right?"

"Exactly," I said.

The ball expanded in Blue's hands until he had to cradle it like it was a big, round baby.

"Not sure how to make it any bigger," Blue said.

"Think of it going through and around you," I said. "It's like you're the gum in the middle of a monster Blow Pop."

"Mmmm," Blue said. "I love Blow Pops."

"Yeah," Andi said. "Especially when you still have candy stuck to your teeth and it mixes with the gum."

Blue smiled. "Oh, yeah."

The ball swelled until it was up against Blue's face. He took in a big breath and held it, then slammed his head through the ball. It expanded more and surrounded him. A few seconds later, he started yelling.

"Blue, you okay?" I yelled.

"Yeah, I'm fine. Just got a little excited."

"Keep going," I said. "Big enough to hold us all."

The water bulged and grew to the size of the storage shed in my backyard.

"Come on in," Blue said.

I moved forward and stepped through with everyone right behind me. We stood in the center of the water Blow Pop, but something still felt wrong.

I looked down and saw that everybody's feet were still

on the ground and the water ball was surrounding our ankles.

"How do we stay inside?" Brianna asked.

"Blue," I said. "Can you toughen the outside?"

He wiggled his fingers and I felt the water thicken around my ankles, but it wasn't solid enough to step on.

"Maybe it just needs some texture," Andi said as she rubbed the bottom of her nose.

She sneezed and shot a big green puddle at her toes. It hit the water and she spread it around with her feet and then stepped on it. It held.

Andi slid around and her lily pad of snot moved with her.

"Nice," she said just before letting out more sneezes at our feet.

"Ewww," Brianna said. "I'm not sticking my . . ."

"Brianna," I said. "Bravery, remember?"

Cal reached over and spread it around her feet.

He winked at her. "It's like we're swapping spit."

Brianna crossed her arms. "Not even in the afterlife."

He looked down.

"Okay," she said. "Maybe in the afterlife if nothing better was around."

Cal smiled. "If that's your way of saying thank you, I'll take it."

Brianna stepped on her snot pad like it was radioactive.

"Being dead has some advantages," she said. "It doesn't seem like I can puke."

"All right," Cal said. "We're all ready, so let's get this bubble boat moving."

"How do I do that?" Blue asked.

Cal shrugged. "Make it spin, I guess."

Blue cupped his hands together and moved them around like he was holding an invisible joystick. The bubble moved forward and our snot pads stayed in place, floating on the spinning water shell.

We moved further into the lake. The water rose as we eased down the underwater sand, moving deeper until the dark green water surrounded us. We reached the edge of the sand and as our bubble inched over the edge, it fell.

We floated down quickly and caught up to the orb that was waiting below. It pulsated and didn't flinch as we passed it by.

"We're going to fall into the bottomless pit!" Blue yelled.

"Spin faster, Blue," I said calmly. "Just keep spinning."

Blue slapped his hands back into joystick mode and twisted them faster. The bubble responded and we stopped falling.

"We're stable," I said. "Can you make us move back towards the guide?"

Blue nodded and shifted his hands forward. We rose and moved forward and reached the orb. As we approached, our pulsating guide drifted on, leading the way.

We followed in a straight line, but as the orb took his first turn to the left, we shifted right.

"Blue . . ." Brianna said.

"I know, I know," he said. "Just getting a feel for it."

We took a long circle around and the orb was waiting. It took off again once we were back in line.

We neared a black mass that looked like the bottom of an iceberg made of tar. The orb moved around it and Blue followed. One glacier turned into three, then kept increasing until we were surround by them.

The orb didn't pause and neither did Blue. He kept focused on the guide and the rest of us kept quiet to let him concentrate.

We traveled for more than twenty minutes when the tar glaciers disappeared.

The orb stopped and turned.

"We are beyond the obstacles of Tar Lake. You only have to reach the surface and the black sand of Tartenna will be visible. I have fulfilled my duty."

The orb pulsed brightly and then disappeared.

Our vessel stood still and we all turned toward Blue.

He shrugged. "Now what?"

CHAPTER 15:
RESCUE

"Just keep going forward," I said. "If we're close, we should see something."

We moved a few more yards and could see the dark shape of the land ahead.

"Looks like we're almost there," I said. "You can start moving up toward the shore."

We angled upwards and saw several dark shadows near the surface. One of the shadows moved. It got bigger as we closed in and looked like it was heading directly for us.

"What is that?" Blue asked.

"I don't know," I said. "But you might want to avoid it."

Blue shifted us left but the object followed. It closed in. It shot at us and spun around our water ship.

The shadow that was stalking us looked like a big prehistoric fish. It was larger than our bubble and parts of it were transparent. Inside its body we could see its skeleton and it had neon pink eyes that glowed in the dark water.

It swam by again and opened its gaping mouth, revealing eight long fangs.

"Can you get us out of here?" I asked.

Blue hands were twitching. "I'm trying."

We backed away but were no match for the speed of the fang fish.

"We need some nitro to get this thing moving," Cal said.

"Right," I said. "We need a boost."

I looked at my friends, trying to think of something. "Brianna, I think you can help us."

Her eyes bulged and she stared at me without saying a word.

"Spit your fire behind us as hard as you can. If it's fast enough, maybe it'll give us some speed."

Brianna closed her eyes, hocked back and spit. A thin line of fire flew through the bubble and we moved forward a little faster. She immediately covered her mouth with her hand.

"That's great, Brianna," I said. "Can you keep the flame going? Maybe try not to cover your mouth afterwards. We don't mind if it's bad manners."

The fang fish swooped by and chomped down on the bubble. Blue turned the bubble as the fangs pierced through. The bite scraped my shoulder and gashed a small piece of my skin. There wasn't any blood, but I felt sharp pinpricks in the wound.

I tried to stifle a scream so I wouldn't scare anyone.

"You felt that?" Andi asked.

My face must have given me away.

"Yes, it hurt. I guess Craver and Conniver aren't the only things that can cause pain."

Cal looked up. "It's coming back!"

I turned to Brianna. "Please try, Bree. I don't know

what else to do."

She nodded and tightened her fists. She leaned her head back and snorted like my father used to while he slept. She threw her head forward and a thick flame flew out of her mouth. Instead of stopping, she continued blowing it out.

We all shifted back as the bubble jumped forward. We flew past the fang fish, heading straight for the underwater part of the shoreline.

"Take us up, Blue," I said. "Don't want to slam into the shore."

The flame died and we started to slow down. Brianna didn't hesitate. She hocked back and threw another fire blast. Blue turned us upwards.

We had company. Five more fang fish were heading toward us.

"Just keep going," Cal said. "Barrel right through them like a bowling ball. Brianna, we need another strong one."

Brianna jammed her fists into her stomach as she took in a deep breath. I felt the heat as a loud, bright blue flame flew from her mouth.

We shot past the group of fang fish and only one remained. It opened its jaws and we slammed into its face as we flew up and out of the water, taking it with us.

We were airborne and moving fast as the fang fish fell back down to the water. We slowed down and then started to fall. I could see black sand below. The bubble splashed apart as we hit the ground and everything went black.

I shook my head and pulled up, realizing my face was in the sand. I spit out and checked everybody around me.

"Everybody okay?"

"Excellent!" Cal was jumping as he ran for his arm, which was a few yards away. "That was the ultimate cannon ball."

"Grim!" Andi yelled as she ran past us.

We looked up and Grim was floating at the edge of the sand. His head was down and we couldn't see his face.

We ran to him, but he didn't move.

"Grim, what's wrong?" I asked.

He looked up. "I am not the true Reaper. I am only an extension."

When we first arrived Grim had mentioned he couldn't generate any more incarnations of himself after the souls stopped passing. Something must have changed.

"Can you take us to him?" I asked.

The reaper raised his arm and extended a bony finger. "He is weak and I will soon disappear. Go that way."

We stepped out of the sand and onto the ground. The cracked surface was like a black, jagged tile that clicked with every step. I stared at the empty horizon.

"We need to hurry," I said.

Cal broke into a run and we all followed.

A fog appeared ahead. We heard a whooshing sound and Cal stopped.

"See those blue things?" he asked.

As we moved closer, there were five or six patches of blue fog scattered around us. I looked at the one furthest away and saw a familiar shape.

"There," I pointed. "That's him."

We rushed toward Grim. He hovered over a black mound of melted lava below him as the center burned at his feet. A blue mist engulfed him.

Andi reached out and grabbed his arm. "Mr. Grim?"

He didn't react.

"I don't think he can hear me," Andi said.

I kicked at the black lava. "Maybe the mist coming out of this thing has him in some kind of trance."

I kicked harder and a small piece chipped off. Cal started kicking, too and then Andi joined in. The mound fell apart with each kick until it left a gaping hole in the ground that glowed with a blue flame that the mist rose from.

"I'll stop it up," Andi said as she tickled her nose.

She heaved and let out a big sneeze. The goo hit the hole and filled it. It immediately started to bubble, but the mist disappeared.

Grim fell to the ground.

"Help me pull him away in case the mist breaks back through," I told Cal.

We grabbed Grim and dragged him off as the bubbles on the seal of snot started popping.

"Thank you," Grim mumbled. "Thank you for coming for me. It took my last bit of energy to send a reaper to you once I sensed you at the edge of the water. I'm still not even sure how I got here. The last thing I remember was talking to Elvis."

"What about opening the portal?" I asked.

Grim's head tilted. "What portal?"

"The portal we used to escape."

"Portals open to Underworlders when they need them, but I did not do that. Your desire to leave at that moment must have triggered it. What did you escape from?"

I told him about Craver and Conniver and our desperate exit in the convertible.

"Time," Grim said. "They've had a long time to find a way to remove everything in their path, including me."

"They said they were heading to the Feast," I said. "We weren't sure what to do considering they stomped us pretty bad."

Grim nodded. "They may have planned on keeping me and any other Underworlders away while they had their soul feast, but the one thing they didn't plan for was all of you. It's time to find out why you were brought here."

We moved back to the lake where Blue formed another monster sized blue bubble.

"All aboard," he yelled from within.

I walked into Grim's back as he stopped. The rattling of his bones was unnerving.

"What's wrong," I asked.

"I can't step any further," Grim said.

"That's why the Oracle couldn't come with us. Craver and Conniver set up some kind of protection spell and she couldn't come into the lake, either."

"She wanted to, though," Brianna said.

Grim's head turned. "The Oracle wanted to save me?"

"Yes, she did," Brianna said as she crossed her arms. "She's beautiful, smart and still wanted to save you even after everything you did to her. What a horrible woman."

"Brianna, more important things going on here than Grim's love life," I said. "Grim, what do we do? We came all this way for you."

"Get to the Oracle and get to Purgatory. I was barely able to send a reaper to you when you arrived, but I don't know if my power is limited to Tartenna. Maybe the brothers never expected my escape. Once I can gather my strength, I will try to send another reaper to you if I am able."

I turned to Cal, Andi and Brianna. "Everybody get in the bubble, please. I'll be right there."

No one argued. Once everyone was inside, I turned back to Death.

"Grim, I don't know how we're going to do this. I know you think we were brought here for a reason, but I still have no power."

Grim put his bony hand on my shoulder. "Grey, even if you don't end up shooting balls of water or sneezing out green snot, you have the respect of the rest of your friends there. You're the captain of this crew. They don't need you to fight for them, they just need you to lead them."

I let out a big breath. I still had no clue what was about to happen, but I knew we were the only ones who had any chance of stopping it.

"Thanks, Grim. It's pretty amazing that I went from riding my bike a few weeks ago to being friends with Death himself."

Grim's head tilted. "Friends? You actually consider me a friend?"

I nodded. "Only a friend can make me feel better when I'm nervous, and although I haven't felt much since I've been here, my stomach's been in a knot the last few hours. I'm actually okay now. I just wanted to say thanks in case I don't get another chance."

I walked into the bubble. I saw Grim's face before we descended into the lake and although I'm sure he'd deny it, I swear I saw him smile.

CHAPTER 16:
CONFRONTATION

The bubble burst as we arrived back at the Tar Lake shore where we started our rescue mission.

The Oracle stood with her hands against the invisible shield that kept her from entering the lake. She looked around and behind us as we moved toward her.

I crossed past the shield and the Oracle grabbed me by my shoulders. "Where is Grimmy?"

"We found him and he's fine, but he's stuck like you are and couldn't come with us. We have to get to Purgatory. He's going to try and send us a reaper if he can."

Her grip loosened. "So, he's really okay?"

Brianna grabbed her hands. "He's fine, Oracle. I promise."

The Oracle's eyes welled up and her top lip quivered.

"Oracle," I said. "Can you focus and see if you can tell exactly where Craver and Conniver are?"

She nodded and rubbed her face. Her lip stopped quivering and she closed her eyes.

"They are definitely in Purgatory," she said. "I can't tell

where exactly but I sense fear and screaming souls. You just need to follow the chaos and they should be near."

"We can't wait any more, then," I said. "Let's get to the car."

I jumped in the front seat with Andi in the middle and the Oracle back at the wheel. The Oracle revved the engine and raised her hand. A hole opened up ahead of us.

None of us spoke as we raced through. Something was different. We didn't come out immediately like we had all the previous times, we were just surrounded in darkness with wind blowing in our faces.

The Oracle screamed. She turned to me and her face started to blur as if the wind were pressing the colors of her face back.

"Can't go on . . ." she said as she disappeared.

The car started to spin and I grabbed the wheel. Cal leapt from the back seat and took over.

The car stabilized and we jumped out. We were back in the Old West town where we had first arrived, parked in front of the saloon.

"What are we doing back here?" Andi asked. "This isn't Purgatory."

"Maybe we can't get there directly," I said. "But this is where we all arrived. Hopefully we're close."

Bright red and orange flashes appeared in the dark horizon.

A few seconds later we heard a booming thunder mixed with screams.

"Something's going on over there," Blue said.

"Sounds like chaos to me," I said. "That must be the place."

"Then let's move," Cal said as he jumped in the car. He hit the gas pedal, but nothing happened.

Andi slammed the passenger door shut. "Looks like this

is as far as the convertible goes, too."

"How are we going to get there?" Cal asked. "If we walk it might be over by the time we make it."

"I have some appropriate transportation I can provide," a familiar voice said.

Grim hovered behind us. The reaper looked exactly like him, but it had a dull glow around its robe.

"Grim, you did it," I said.

"It seems like this is the only other place I can appear right now. You'll have to get there on your own. The car . . ."

Grim's new reaper paused as he looked the car up and down.

"What did you do to my car?" he growled.

"We had an accident escaping Craver and Conniver," I said. "Can't you fix it?"

"Yes, but that's not the point. It's not easy to find a body shop guy in the Underworld. I worked on that for . . ."

"Forget about the car," Brianna said. "More important things than guy stuff here."

Grim looked back at us. "Yes, you're right. I guess the destruction of the Underworld is a little more pressing."

I tried to get him back on track. "So, you were saying about the car?"

"Yes, the car. It appears the car is part of the enchantment and you can't use it to get to Purgatory."

"Then what did you mean by appropriate transportation?" I asked.

Grim's hands rose and he tapped his fingertips together. "We are in the Old West."

The ground shook and a parade of stomping sounds got closer. From behind the building five skeletal horses galloped toward us and stopped.

"Wow," Brianna said. "I had horses, but they had skin. How are we going to sit on these?"

"Check the saloon," Grim said.

We ran in and found saddles decorating the walls. We each grabbed one and came back to the horses.

Andi and Blue stared at the saddles and looked back at me.

"No idea," I said. "I haven't been on a horse since I was seven, but it was on a merry-go-round."

"No problem," Cal said. "I'm sure Brianna and I can help. I ride horses at my uncle's ranch all the time."

"Don't worry if you've never ridden," Grim said. "The horses will know the way. You just need to hang on."

Cal and Brianna helped us set up the saddles. I helped Andi on her horse and then walked up to mine.

"Cal, can I get some help here?" I asked after I slipped three times trying to get my foot in one of the saddle straps.

Cal gave me a boost and then helped Blue. Brianna was already on her horse.

"You are all ready," Grim said. "Do what you need to do."

"You know how to ride these, Cal," I said. "Want to lead the way?"

"Nah, man. Grim said they'll drive themselves. This is your cavalry, buddy."

I smiled. "Let's go, then. Hyah!"

My horse jumped forward and the rest followed. The galloping and the rush of seeing Purgatory getting closer was overwhelming. The horses moved almost as fast as the convertible. Flashes from Purgatory grew closer and within a few minutes we could hear the commotion within.

The horses stopped near a wall made of black and white stones.

In the center of the wall was a glowing doorway the size

of a big garage door. We dismounted and stood in front of the entrance.

I looked at my companions. "Everybody ready?"

Cal and Andi nodded, followed by Blue. Brianna didn't move and had her hands cupped around her mouth.

"Brianna," I said. "We'll be with you."

She lowered her head and took in a quick breath. "I'm ready."

I stepped through the doorway.

It wasn't what I expected. I thought it would be as dark and gloomy as most of what we've seen, but instead it was bright. There were blue and yellow flowers on one side and a fountain in front of us. A grassy hill rose behind it. It looked peaceful, although it sounded like a warzone behind the hill.

I rushed up the hill with everyone behind me. I looked down into an open valley filled with people. It looked like a sold-out outdoor concert. Everyone looked like us, but their nearly transparent bodies glowed. We were solid and looked a little paler than when we were alive, but they looked like full bodied ghosts.

"Are those souls?" Andi asked.

"I think so," I said.

It was wall-to-wall people. Some were talking and others were exploring their surroundings, but most stood silently. To the back right of my view, I saw waves of movement as souls ran in all directions. There were bright flashes every few seconds mixed with moans and yells.

"That must be where they are," I said, pointing to the commotion. "Stay together."

I started moving. We ran into a wall of souls as we reached the bottom of the hill. I hesitated as several of them glared at us. One woman waved, but most just moved aside. I moved faster. The souls all turned as we passed, but remained calm as if nothing was happening.

As we moved through the thickness of the bodies, I saw panic in some of the soul's eyes. The flashes and yells were closer. The space between the bodies increased until we reached a clear patch of grass. Souls had spread out and formed an open circle. I looked in the direction they were staring and noticed a familiar canine shape.

Craver's blood-red body was on top of a man lying face up, gnawing at him as the man's arms flailed. Craver bit and pulled, but there was no blood. With each bite, the same blue, glowing mass of soul like he had tried to take from me filled his mouth. As he swallowed, I saw the glow go down his throat and into his stomach before it faded.

Craver snapped four more times and on the last swallow, the man dissipated and screamed. The blue glow in Craver's stomach turned into a bright orange flash. He howled as he moved towards the next soul, a teenage girl who tried to run away. Craver jammed his head across her legs and she fell. She looked up and froze. She was trapped.

"We have to save her," I said.

Everyone circled near Craver as he chomped down on the girl.

"Now's the time," I said. "Blue, hit him with a water bomb. Just a small one to get started."

Blue looked at me with his eyes bulging, but didn't move. Brianna had her hands clasped and Cal was walking side to side, but not doing anything.

I turned to Andi.

She looked at me and winked. "I'll get this party started."

Craver had just pulled his first piece of the teenager's soul when Andi sneezed and hit him in the mouth with a blast of snot.

Craver yelped and turned around.

"More for feast," he growled as he leapt at Andi.

She closed her eyes and held her hand out to protect her face.

Craver landed on her chest and knocked her to the ground. I ran to kick him, but before I got there, Cal had already dove on his red body.

He knocked Craver on his side and stood over him. He started punching. Craver's face turned as Cal hit him on his bat snout, then he snapped at Cal's arm and locked his jaw. He threw his neck sideways and Cal's arm went flying.

A shot of water blasted Craver's side. Blue hit him with a few more small water balls, but they seemed to annoy the beast more than hurt him.

Craver bit on Cal's chest and latched on. The reaction was different. Unlike the souls he had just attacked, his teeth were embedded in Cal's flesh and Cal yelled like he felt it. There still wasn't any blood, but it looked painful.

Without thinking, I rushed in and kicked Craver's side. He wouldn't let go and bit down harder.

Blue gave up on his bombs and started kicking. "Leave him alone!"

Craver jumped back and hunched down on all fours. He kept his grip on Cal and pulled him back. Blue and I kept kicking as Cal struggled to get free.

Craver let go, flashed his teeth and then bit down again. Just as his fangs were about to gnash into Cal's shoulder, an orange flame hit him in the eyes. He jumped back and cried like an injured dog.

I turned back and saw Brianna staring at Craver with smoke coming out of her mouth.

She ran to Cal. "Are you okay?"

He grabbed at his chest. "I'm fine now, but man, that did not feel good."

Craver was rubbing his face in the grass.

"Keep hitting him now that he's hurt," I said.

Cal sat up and grabbed his right arm. He flung it at Craver with his left and it smacked the bat-wolf on the body, then boomeranged back to him.

Blue cupped his hands and started firing water balls, but this time they were bigger and faster. Each blast knocked Craver back a step. He tried to run away, but a snot shot from Andi hit his feet and he struggled to break free.

"Get him, Bree," I said.

She snorted and hit him with a fat flame right on the face. Craver struggled to move and moaned as each hit kept coming.

"We've got him," Cal said, just as he fell forward and landed on his face.

Conniver had leapt on Cal's back, then turned and jumped on Brianna. She screamed and her flame died in mid-stream as Conniver bit her neck. He snapped at Andi and Blue, stopping their water and snot attack. He rushed to Craver and licked him on the face.

"You think you can finish my brother so easily?" Conniver snorted. "I do not know how you were able to get here, but see how you do against us both."

He jumped at Cal, took a bite, then jumped on Blue and snapped at his back. Brianna was still on the ground grabbing her neck.

"Keep attacking," I said. "Just keep doing what you were doing."

Andi sneezed and a green blast shot in the air. Conniver rolled out of the way and the snot hit Blue instead. Conniver got to his feet and jumped at Andi.

I ran to help Andi, but a piercing pain filled my shoulder. Craver had jumped from behind and sunk his fangs into me. He dragged me back.

Conniver walked from Andi and stood in front of

Brianna. "My young beauty, do you see the large hill behind me?"

He craned his head back toward the hill that looked more like a steep mountain. There was a faint glow above it.

"The souls there take time to reach. You and the waterboy are going to help me destroy that hill and bring the souls down here to us."

"Why would I do that?" Brianna asked. "I won't help you."

"Refuse and I'll rip the boy with the loose arms and legs to shreds."

Cal looked up. "Don't worry about me, Brianna. Don't even think about it."

"He's tougher than I am," she said. "I won't help you."

Conniver laughed. "I spent centuries preparing for everything, Little Princess. You and your friends were unexpected, but I picked up an artifact back in Tartenna that makes all of you insignificant. You will do as I say."

Something started glowing on Conniver's neck. I hadn't noticed before but he wore a necklace that blended with his marble fur. It looked like it was made of black bones, but it had a pendant in the shape of a snake's head. The pendant's eyes were glowing.

"Fire!" Conniver yelled.

Brianna's head jumped forward and a blast of flame bigger than anything she'd ever produced flew from her mouth and struck the hill.

As the fireball hit and pieces of the hill went flying, my insides felt like I had been punched.

"What are you doing, Brianna?" Andi said.

"It wasn't me," she yelled back.

"Let's try you now, waterboy," Conniver said as his pendant glowed brighter.

Blue's hands yanked forward and a succession of basketball-sized water balls flew from him.

Conniver had full control of their abilities.

The blasts hit the hill and it exploded with each strike. My body shook with each impact. I didn't know what Craver had done, but when the pain ended I looked up and he wasn't near me. He had run off and joined his brother.

What was wrong with me? Maybe Conniver's necklace was hitting me with pain since I had no special power. I looked at him and his eyes were closed like it was taking all of his concentration to control the blast of fire and water.

More water and fire blasts came out and I felt more shots of pain all over. I managed to look up.

"Cal," I said. "Use Bree and Blue against them."

Cal shrugged at me. "How do I do that?"

"Move them!"

I fell to my knees as the pain worsened.

Cal jumped up and picked up Bree. Cal turned her body and the balls of flame shifted until they hit Craver and knocked him off his feet.

Andi moved to Blue and turned him until his water blasts hit Conniver. The blasts stopped coming as Conniver lost his concentration.

The pain in my body let up and I joined my friends.

I turned to Brianna and Blue. "Keep them coming."

"I can't make them as big as Conniver did," she said.

"Just think of what it felt like," I said. "Try everything you can to get that feeling back."

She took in a few quick breaths and let out a blue flame that smacked Craver, who was still on the ground.

"Keep going," I said.

She let out another flame that intensified as it continued to strike. The bat-wolf bellowed loud enough to echo through the entire valley, then his red body exploded into black ash.

"Brother!" Conniver yelled, getting back to his feet.

He ran and sniffed at the dark patch in the grass.

"Take him out, too," I said.

The barrage continued and hit Conniver in one large blast. A ball of flame consumed him and a blast from Blue made it hiss and disappear. When the smoke cleared, a second black patch of burned grass is all that was left.

"We did it!" Brianna yelled. "They're gone."

She hugged Cal and Blue high-fived Andi.

I didn't move. I kept looking at the burned ground. I wasn't sure why, but I felt this wasn't over. I walked over to the patches and rubbed my hand in them, picking up a pinch of hot ash.

I let the black dust fall off my hand and it flew up in the air as if guided by a whirlwind. The ash spun and darkened. A heavy set of claws hit me. I looked up and Craver and Conniver were staring back at me.

"Did the Oracle not tell you how this works?" Conniver said. "We were removed from our father's essence and imprisoned because the Underworld couldn't destroy us. What makes you think you can, you ignorant souls?"

His necklace glowed and Brianna and Blue shot their blasts at the hill. I looked up as the pain returned and a big chunk of the hill shaped like a boot fell towards me. I rolled to the side as my forearm burned in pain. I pulled up my sleeve and looked at my arm. A patch of skin turned red and formed into the same boot shape as the piece of the hill. The chunk crashed to the ground and the burning on my arm spread. The heat was so bad I jumped down and rubbed my arm on the grass.

The pain eased and I heard more noise. I looked up and saw souls falling off the hill. They landed safely, but Craver and Conniver were waiting.

Blue tried to hit them again but Conniver lifted his head and the water bombs turned and hit the hill harmlessly instead.

"What do we do now?" Andi asked. "They're not even fighting back."

I walked back to the group.

"They don't think we're a threat anymore," I said. "Everybody okay?"

"Other than the fact we just gave them some fresh souls to feed on, I'd say we're great," Cal said. "We beat them, but they just came back. We can't win."

I looked at my friends and realized Cal was right.

CHAPTER 17:
ENLIGHTENMENT

Brianna stared at her feet. Blue and Cal gaped blankly at Craver and Conniver feasting.

"Are we just going to stand here and do nothing?" Andi asked.

"What do you want us to do?" Cal asked. "Sometimes the other team is just better. We're done."

Andi ran toward the mound of shattered boot-shaped dirt chunks and kicked a piece towards the beasts. They paid no notice but my arm flared again.

I rubbed the spot. If Craver and Conniver were totally ignoring us, then why did it still hurt? I checked the matching red mark on my arm and looked back at the mound. I walked over and stomped a piece. The mark on my arm swelled as my shoe crushed the dirt.

"Bree," I said. "Can you hit the hill again?"

She shook her head. "They'll just use it against us."

"I don't think they will as long as we don't try to hurt them. Just aim for the hill. Not too much force this time, though. Please."

Brianna's nostrils flared but she didn't argue. She hocked back quietly and sent a flame flying. It hit a small part off the hill and I felt a light burning sensation on my back as a few pieces of dirt fell.

I closed my eyes and concentrated on the pain. I let it spread and I'm not sure how, exactly, but I sensed the entire hill. I felt its loss as the pieces of dirt flew off as if they were something inside my own body that had been shot out of my back. It was like I could feel the hill breathing.

"What's going on, Grey?" Cal asked. "Quit messing around."

I ignored him.

"Bree, hit it harder," I said.

"You're wasting time," Cal said.

"No," Bree interrupted. "He's got something."

She turned and slammed the hill with a strong blast. The target shattered and I doubled over. I felt my insides break, but I was able to fight back and isolate the throbbing sensation.

I twisted my torso to the side, trying to push the pain away from me. Part of the hill turned and flew towards the spot where Craver and Conniver were feasting. The pieces slammed into them and exploded.

I was able to focus and felt the pieces of hill that had already fallen to the ground. I willed them up and out and they came at the Sons of Elvis ten times faster than when they fell.

"How are you doing that?" Blue asked.

"Don't know," I grumbled, still trying to stifle the pain.

"Doesn't matter how," Cal said. "Just keep doing it. We may have one last bat after all"

Pieces kept flying and hitting their faces and bodies. Conniver tried to get up and his necklace glowed, but each time he tried to move, debris struck him. He finally fell to the ground and he and his brother kept falling back.

Conniver was moving wildly, trying to avoid being hit.

"It's the powerless boy," he yelled. "He's doing this!"

Brianna sent a flame into Conniver and Blue followed with a monster blast. Conniver detonated on impact.

We kept the attack on Craver. A ball of wet ash spun and Conniver reappeared next to him.

"Nothing you do matters. Not even if you control the ground itself. Keep doing what you're doing. We will just come back and feast. We cannot be destroyed."

Craver jumped back up and dove into the mass of running souls.

I sent another piece of ground at Conniver, but he jumped out of the way and ran towards Andi. He knocked her down and stood on her body, but didn't attack.

"Hit me now, boy," he growled. "You can help me finish off your friend."

I couldn't hit him without striking Andi.

"You've all failed. My brother and I will do what our father never could. We will consume enough souls to take back the Underworld and will never be imprisoned again. If any soul wants to pass on to the next life, they'll have to get through us."

He was right. They were about to finish what their father started. Their father . . . Memphus . . . Elvis . . .

I clenched my fists and concentrated. In the distance there was a booming sound that was louder than the chaos we were standing in. I felt the surge in my chest.

"Craver," Conniver yelled. "Take care of that boy. I don't know what he's doing, but stop him. I almost have enough souls."

Craver's claws slashed my face and I fell. I shifted my focus and threw a cloud of debris at him, but he was so close I got hit just as hard. Not my best idea.

I punched and kicked at Craver's head, but it didn't bother him. He slammed his fangs into my collarbone and it felt like I'd been stabbed with a hot kitchen knife.

"Keep them off of him," Andi said.

She hit Craver in the eye with a snot ball that was quickly followed by fire and water. Craver jumped off me and looked up as more flames and water came at him. The shots shifted away in mid-air. I looked back and saw Conniver and his glowing necklace.

"Over there," I called out to Cal, pointing toward Conniver.

"Toss me one of those water baseballs, Blue," Cal said. "And thicken it up."

He pulled off his right leg and hopped to keep his balance. He spun his leg and eased it on his shoulder.

Blue tossed him a water ball and Cal swung his leg like a baseball bat, putting his full weight into it. His swing blurred as his leg flung around and hammered its target. The ball looked like a tiny comet as it whisked in the air and hit Conniver's side.

"Keep going and keep shooting at him," Cal said. "If we hit him hard and fast enough to keep him moving, he might not be able to concentrate on all of us."

Andi and Brianna continued their barrage at Craver as Blue tossed several balls back at Cal.

Cal hit a few balls at Conniver and then turned to Craver. He kept Conniver moving so he couldn't control the rest of our attacks.

I clenched my fists again and I shut everything out.

I felt it. The rumbling in the distance grew closer until a massive shadow busted through the Purgatory entrance and hovered above us.

I eased it down and as it hit the ground, everyone

stopped fighting.

I had just moved a mountain.

Elvis the Memphus was before us. He craned his head and neck down to see what was happening.

"What have you done, my sons?" Elvis asked.

"Done?" Conniver said. "We've done what you could not, Father. We almost have enough souls to take the Underworld back. We will not give up as you did and be forced to surrender to the age of humans."

Elvis ignored them and turned to me. "Why am I here?"

"They were a part of you," I said. "They have to be stopped, Elvis, but we can't destroy them. Can you take them back?"

Elvis' long neck craned toward Craver and Conniver. "I may be able to change their form or reabsorb them, but they are my sons and a part of me. I cannot risk harming them."

Conniver laughed deep and loud enough to echo throughout Purgatory.

"It's finished, boy. We only need a few more souls to finish the feast and I think we'll take them now."

He leapt back into the crowd and took down the closest soul. Craver followed.

"Elvis," I said. "You have to do this. What happens if they take everything over?"

The Memphus turned away from me. "I cannot destroy my own."

"But you told me they couldn't be destroyed, anyway. That's why they became what they are now and were imprisoned, right?"

I was interrupted by a huge flash that came out of the last soul Conniver extinguished. The light was filled with an electric charge of lightning that cracked and shot out of the crowd.

"Yes," Conniver shouted. "It is done."

He walked out of the crowd with Craver by his side.

"Throw me one," Cal said. Blue tossed up a water ball and Cal smacked it, but with a flick of his head, Conniver made it fly past.

Andi, Blue and Brianna attacked, but everything changed course before it hit anything.

"This is over," Conniver said. "The Underworld is ours to take. I think I'll start with the Oracle."

I looked at my team. Cal had his head down and Blue was shaking his head. Brianna's hands were covering her face.

I looked at Andi. Her fists were clenched tight and she had a scowl on her face. She was angry and defiant, even now.

I liked her reaction best.

I broke into a run towards the brothers. "Come on!"

I dove on Conniver and wrapped my arms around his body. He shook me off, but I kept on punching. Andi jumped behind and did the same.

As Conniver turned, I saw Cal, Blue and even Brianna on top of Craver.

Conniver flipped me to the ground and slammed his front claws in my chest, slowly digging them in.

"Still so foolish, boy. You couldn't stop us and our father won't stop us. You'll be the first Underworlder to suffer the fate of having your essence removed as my brother and I did so many years ago."

He bit into my chest and pulled out a chunk of my flesh. It was glowing blue. My breath sucked in and I couldn't breathe out.

He'd finally taken a piece of my soul.

Andi kicked, Brianna shot flames and Cal hit water baseballs at us, but he didn't flinch. Craver kept them back and they watched as Conniver took another bite.

I yelled as I was finally able to breathe.

"Elvis, just take them back. You don't have to destroy them!"

He didn't look back at me. "I am sorry."

"Your soul is mine, grey-eyed one," Conniver said. "Just one more bite."

My insides burned and I felt anger, fear and pain all at the same time. I felt Elvis' essence and held it. I threw my arms out and pulled back like I had an invisible rope. Elvis' head snapped back and struck Craver and Conniver, knocking them to the ground.

"No," Elvis said. "I cannot . . ."

My body twisted and I closed my eyes tight. It felt like my head was going to explode. I clasped my hands and then pulled them apart, forcing Elvis' mouth open.

"Help him, Blue," Andi said.

Blue shot a stream of water at Craver, knocking him forward. I moved Elvis' open mouth closer until it was just above his sons.

"Blue," Cal yelled. "Make it like our lake ship!"

Blue nodded and shot two larger spheres of water that surrounded Craver and Conniver.

Blue turned to Andi. "Your turn."

She hit the balls with snot to make the brothers stick.

"Brianna," I yelled, "Make it spin."

She shot a thin flame under the water balls and they turned, moving up but away from Elvis. Cal picked up his leg and smacked the trapped brothers, knocking them in the right direction.

I clapped my hands and Elvis' mouth shut around the spheres, splattering water as they ripped apart. I threw my hands up again and Elvis' head rose to the air, allowing his sons to fall down his throat.

I stood up and let go of my grip on the Memphus.

"They're not dead, Elvis. I know you can feel them. Just try to change what they are. You won't hurt them."

Elvis' head shook. "You don't know that for certain. I could destroy them and this time, the Underworld Council won't be as forgiving."

His hotel-sized belly glowed red.

"The souls," Elvis said. "I can smell them."

"Your craving must have returned now that they're inside you," I said. "Get rid of them before they take you over."

Elvis' neck stretched down into the crowd and he sniffed at the nearby souls.

I grabbed my chest as I felt the conflict within him.

"I'm trying to help you, Elvis," I said. "And I need your help, too. You can go back to being the mountain again, helping everyone else in the Underworld. You said you were happy there."

Elvis didn't turn.

"It's not working," Cal said.

He was right.

I pulled Elvis' neck back and over me.

"Give me a boost," I said.

Cal moved toward me but Andi put her arm in front of him. "What are you doing, Grey?"

"I have to get inside and do this myself. I don't know any other way."

Elvis's body shook and the ground rumbled. Pieces of the mountain dirt on his stomach shed loose.

"They're trying to get out. Do it, Cal."

Cal held out his hands and boosted me into Elvis' mouth. I crawled up and then willed his head up.

I slid down his throat like it was a water slide. The red glow got brighter as I moved down and then I slammed into Craver and Conniver. We were in the belly of Elvis and there was enough room to hold my house as well as half my neighborhood block.

Craver and Conniver looked weak, but they were on their feet.

"This isn't over," Conniver said. "We will escape and finish this."

Craver eased towards me and flung his red spiked tail at my head. I ducked, but it hit my ear and stung.

I looked around me and saw pieces of the hotel caves scattered around me. I picked up a lamp in a pumpkin shape and smashed it on Craver's snout. He yelped and jumped back.

I stood up and found a painting of the Eiffel Tower. I threw it like a Frisbee and it flew by Conniver's head.

"Paintings and lamps won't stop us," he hissed.

The brothers moved slowly toward me.

I twisted my neck and felt each joint in my body creak. The Underworld was vast, but I needed to concentrate. I needed to change and mold these beasts, but I didn't know how. I could sense the brothers were gathering their strength to attack, but I didn't care. I thought of a sculptor and an artist. They created and recreated. Their minds gave them their gift, but they expressed them with the same instrument.

Their hands.

I shifted all that I sensed of the Underworld into my hands.

I opened my eyes and my palms were glowing green.

Craver leapt on me and I grabbed him by the throat. I felt my fingers dig into his neck.

Craver hovered away from me and I saw Conniver's pendant glowing. He was pulling his brother back, but I jumped forward and squeezed my fingers around the necklace.

Conniver flinched and the necklace snapped off his neck.

"Get it back!" he yelled at Craver.

Craver's snout flared. He rushed and bit into my arm. Instead of trying to push him off, I grabbed his throat again.

Conniver growled and stared at the pendant in my hand. He jumped at me and I slammed the pendant into his eye. Before he could react, I let go of Craver and grabbed Conniver's lion nose and squeezed. He howled in pain as I kicked at his brother.

My hands glowed brighter.

They licked at their faces and circled me, preparing for their next attack. I looked at my glowing palms and felt a surge of heat.

"Let's finish this, brother," Conniver said.

"Yes," Craver hissed. "Finish."

They jumped at the same time. As they flew in the air I reached back with both my arms and slammed my palms into their faces. They bit at my hands and without thinking, I shoved each hand into their mouths, letting their fangs slice my arms as I pushed through. My fists went deep into their throats until I felt slimy pouches of goop inside them. I heard souls yelling in my head as I squeezed and felt the pouches burst between my fingers.

Something exploded as my body rattled and everything went black.

CHAPTER 18:
AFTERSHOCK

I heard voices as I felt my entire body throbbing.

"Grey, are you okay?"

It was Andi.

I opened my eyes and everything was blurry at first. I focused and saw Andi standing over me and Brianna kneeling to my side with her hands on my face.

Blue and Cal were nearby.

Cal smiled. "Did you have to go through all that just to get the girls' attention?"

I took Andi's hand and she helped me up.

"About time you woke up, Grey," she said. "You've been out a few hours."

I looked around me and there were black and red pieces of rock scattered everywhere.

"What is all this?" I asked.

Cal picked up a piece. "This? This is what you left of Elvis and his boys. You went in, we heard a fight and then Elvis just exploded."

"Knocked us all back," Blue said. "I flew at least a

hundred yards."

"No," I said. "Elvis wasn't supposed to be destroyed."

"It's okay," a woman's voice said from behind us. It was the Oracle. We turned and she was walking with Grim by her side.

"Elvis is fine," she said.

"The enchantment is broken?" I asked.

"Yes," she said.

"And my souls are moving again," Grim said. "I have some cleanup to do yet, but hopefully all will be back to normal soon."

"Speaking of souls," the Oracle said. "I have something that belongs to each of you."

She raised her hand with her palm up. It glowed and streaks of blue light shot out and hit us each in the chest.

"For keeping your oaths, the Underworld has returned the bargained pieces of your souls."

I felt a sense of relief, but wanted to know everything I had missed. "Are Craver and Conniver gone?"

"Come," the Oracle said. "I'll show you."

"Back to the car?" Andi asked.

"This time you travel the way I do."

She raised her hands and we disappeared in a flash of light. We were back at Rock Mountain Retreat.

The hotel was back in place. There was a rumbling sound followed by Elvis' head coming towards us.

"Thank you, Grey," Elvis said. "You gave me back my life and my sons."

"They're a part of you again?" Andi asked.

"Yes, but not the way they were before."

Elvis craned his neck and aimed his head to the front of his hotel body. Something new was there. It looked like a large gazebo. We moved toward it. Inside was a marble fountain with two twisting designs at the top with alternating water spouts shooting from their tips.

I moved closer.

The spouts were coming from two snouts, one that looked like the face of a lion and another like a bat. Craver and Conniver were molded into these snake-shaped designs and now decorated the fountain.

"My sons are now here with me and can no longer harm anyone. I didn't have to destroy them and you didn't, either. I will never forget that."

"I pictured this right before I blacked out," I said. "I'm not sure how, but I was able to understand how this worked."

"You discovered your power," the Oracle said.

"I'm still not sure exactly what that is."

"It seems you have a special connection to the Underworld. You can sense things and even manipulate the earth. Since Elvis is part of this realm, you were able to sense and become a part of him. Even under the enchantment, I felt you come alive."

"Yes," I said. "When Craver and Conniver tried to destroy the hills inside of Purgatory, I felt the pain of the land. I was able to tune into Elvis and wanted to send him back to his hotel without having to destroy his own sons. So, are you saying I can move mountains whenever I want to now?"

"No. Although Elvis didn't want to harm his offspring, he did want to help. That desire actually gave you the power to move him since at least part of him was willing to try."

"Why don't I sense anything now?"

"Until you realized the connection, it was mostly dormant," the Oracle said. "You had no time to prepare, but by listening to the Underworld you were able to improvise and do what was necessary. I don't think you can sense it now since there is no immediate danger. You can try to refine it for next time."

"Next time?" I said. "How do you know there'll be a next time?"

Grim put his hand on the Oracle's shoulder. "Tell them."

"Yes, but not here. We need a place that's more appropriate."

We said our goodbyes to Elvis and he returned to the solace of his mountain hotel.

With the enchantment lifted, the Oracle raised her hands and teleported us away from Purgatory.

We were back in front of the Old West saloon.

"Let's go inside," the Oracle said.

We entered and my friends and I sat at a table that looked like it could have been filled with cowboys playing poker.

Grim stood next to the Oracle.

"So," I said. "You were talking about a next time?"

The Oracle took in a big breath. "The chaos that Craver and Conniver caused created a rift in the Underworld."

"What kind of rift?" I asked.

"A few entities woke up during the fight and got a taste of the loose soul energy that the feast caused," Grim said. "I'm going to need some help cleaning that mess up."

The Oracle nodded. "There are also some cracks in the Underworld that have given wayward beings easier access to Earth."

"You think we're meant to continue doing more?" Cal asked.

"Yes," the Oracle said. "You weren't just brought here for the short term. You are anomalies of the Underworld and are needed."

"How would that work?" Andi asked. "I mean, would

we all stay together or be broken apart? Would we work for somebody?"

"Grim and I would be your contacts with the Underworld Council. Well, I would. I can't speak for Grim, but he has also been offered the additional duty."

We turned toward our skeletal friend. He looked down.

"My duties are a full-time responsibility," he said. "However, it's been a long time since I have had a new friend down here and I would be honored to continue as a mentor. Plus, I could use some excitement. Death can become stale after a few thousand years. My reapers can handle most of that."

"It's like we're some kind of team or group or something," Blue said. "We need a great name, like the Underworld Avengers."

"How about the Dead Kids?" Andi asked.

We all groaned.

"Even I think that's too grim," Death said.

"The Astros?" Cal suggested.

Brianna shook her head. "No sports names, please."

I remembered what Kristopher had said about being a part of a secret society of the dead. Then I thought how we all got here and everything that happened to get us to this point.

"The Dead Club," I said.

The room was silent. I guess they didn't like it.

Andi smiled. "That has a good ring to it."

Cal, Blue and Brianna were nodding their heads.

"And would the members just be the five of us?" Cal asked.

"I think we'd be the core," I said, "but we could let anyone that helps us be members, too. Like Grim and Oracle."

"Yeah," Andi said. "And if Elvis or the librarian wanted

to be part of it, they could join, too."

Brianna clapped her hands together. "Ooh, we could have memberships and tea party meetings . . ."

The rest of us stared at her.

"All right, I went too far with the tea party. But we could have some kind of membership card or badges or something, right?"

"I don't see why not," the Oracle said. "You might even be able to have the non-dead join as you may be making more trips to the living world."

"Like Kristopher," I said.

She nodded. I already knew he wouldn't hesitate to join.

"Now," the Oracle said, "before we move on, there is still the outstanding matter of acceptance."

"Acceptance?" Blue asked. "What do you mean?"

"You are dead, but must choose to remain an Underworlder."

"So are you saying we have a choice?" Cal said.

"Of course," the Oracle said. "Now that souls are passing through Purgatory again, you can choose to pass on to your next step in the eternal world, or you can stay here and work with us."

I thought about it for about two seconds.

"I'm in. We were all too young to go and this is an opportunity to keep on living. I'd like to help keep the Underworld safe for when my friends and family pass through someday. Eternity will always be there anyway, right?"

"It wouldn't be called eternity if that wasn't the plan," Grim said.

I stood up. "Guys, it's up to all of you to make your own decision, but I hope that everyone stays. No one will hold it against you if you don't, but I think we need to decide now."

"Heck, yeah, I'm staying," Cal said as he stood. "A chance to fight and go on an endless adventure? Sign me up."

Blue had a water ball spinning in his hand. "I'm not going anywhere. Here, I'm almost cool."

Andi looked right at me. "You don't even have to ask. Besides, you think I'm going to let you boys have all the fun?"

We smiled and high-fived, but I realized one voice was absent. I turned back and looked at Brianna. Her eyes were glued to the floor.

"Bree?" I said.

"I'm sorry," she said as she looked up. "I can't stay."

"Why?" Cal asked. "We'll keep you safe, and you did great out there."

"That's not it," she said. "It's my Nana."

"You're leaving because of an old boyfriend named Nana?" Cal asked. "Kind of a girly name, don't you think?"

"My Nana is my grandmother, genius. My mother was so obsessed with these beauty pageants that she didn't have much time to be a mom. My Nana took that job. She died last year, and she told me that she'd see me when my time came and would wait for me. I have to go. I have to know if she's there."

She looked back down and the rest of the crew sat back in their chairs.

"It's okay," I said. "Brianna, you do what you have to do. We'll understand. I can say that I'll miss you and who knows, maybe someday you can come back to us. Right, Oracle?"

"It is extremely rare for anyone to return to the Underworld once they've moved on," the Oracle said. "But I've seen stranger things happen over the last few days."

I moved to Brianna and gave her a hug. Blue and Andi followed me. Cal stood there for a few moments.

"No hug from you, baseball star?" she asked.

"I just don't wanna see you go, Princess. But I get it."

He hugged her and they held their embrace for a long time. As they released, Brianna kissed him on the cheek.

"I'll miss you, too, Cal," she whispered.

She looked at the Oracle. "I'm ready."

The Oracle nodded and pointed to the saloon doors. They flapped open as a white whirlwind formed outside.

"Your path is here," the Oracle said.

Brianna smiled. "Thank you, guys. I hope I see you again someday. Grim, will you do me one favor after I'm gone?"

Grim's eyes shifted. "What kind of favor?"

"Take that beautiful woman out on a date. She deserves it after what she did for you."

If Grim could have blushed I think he would have. "I may already be a step ahead of you on that one."

"He's taking me back to Rock Mountain as soon as things calm down," the Oracle said, almost singing it. "It's just a first step."

"I'm glad," Brianna said. "Everyone deserves to be happy."

She took in a deep breath. "I guess it's time to go."

She turned toward me. "Grey, thank you for believing in me."

"I never doubted you," I said. "We'll miss you, Bree. Take care of yourself."

She walked toward the doors and pulled them open. She turned and waved her princess wave and smiled. She disappeared as she stepped into the whirlwind.

I put my hand on Cal's shoulder. "She'll be okay."

"Yeah, I know she will."

I turned back to Grim and the Oracle.

"I guess we have some important details to discuss," I said. "You know, like your date."

"Funny," Grim said. "Take a moment to let everything sink in. The Underworld's not going anywhere. We can discuss your next mission after we celebrate your first victory."

The Oracle clapped her hands and the table filled with food, sodas and more desserts than I could count. A sundae was dripping chocolate over a mound of strawberries and a brownie the size of a tire sat in the center.

"Wow!" Blue said. "I didn't think we had to eat now that we were dead."

I hadn't thought about it but he was right. We hadn't craved or eaten anything the entire time we had been here.

The Oracle stuck her finger into a huge scoop of chocolate ice cream and tasted it. "We do not need food or drink to survive. The taste of good food is a sense that isn't lost in death. This is for absolute enjoyment."

I smiled as I saw my friends dig into chocolate bars, cookies, gummy worms and every treat they could grab on the table. We laughed and enjoyed ourselves for the brief time we had before embarking on our next adventure.

"To the Dead Club," I said as I raised a piece of cake.

Andi, Cal and Blue raised their desserts and we smashed them together in a toast of pure sugar.

I thought of my parents and Kristopher and had no doubt they would be proud of me and my new friends.

This Dead Club was going to be sweet.

ABOUT THE AUTHOR

Manuel Ruiz[3] was born in Alice, Texas and grew up in nearby Robstown, Texas. He earned his Bachelor of Science degree in Math/Computer Science from Texas A&M University – Kingsville.

Manuel currently lives in Round Rock, Texas with his wife and son where he balances his time around his family, his IT job, his PlayStation and giving the characters in his head something interesting to do.

To learn more about Manuel Ruiz[3] and The Dead Club, please visit:

Website: www.manuelruiz3.com
Facebook: www.facebook.com/ManuelRuizThree